Uth Ink:
Word from the Street

edited by Robin Sokoloski

Playwrights Canada Press
Toronto • Canada

Playwrights Canada Press
The Canadian Drama Publisher
215 Spadina Ave., Suite 230, Toronto, Ontario CANADA M5T 2C7
416.703.0013   fax 416.408.3402
orders@playwrightscanada.com • www.playwrightscanada.com

For professional or amateur production rights, please contact Playwrights Guild of Canada, 210-215 Spadina,Toronto, Ontario M5T 2C7
www.playwrightsguild.ca • info@playwrightsguild.ca
phone 416.703.0201 • fax 416-703-0059

The publisher acknowledges the support of the Canadian taxpayers through the Government of Canada Book Publishing Industry Development Program, the Canada Council for the Arts, the Ontario Arts Council, and the Ontario Media Development Corporation.

Front cover illustrated and designed by Gosia, visit www.gosia.ca.
Production Editor: Robin Sokoloski with JLArt

Library and Archives Canada Cataloguing in Publication

Uth ink : word from the street / Robin Sokoloski, editor.

Anthology of plays from participants in Ottawa, Thunder Bay, Orillia, Etobicoke and Sudbury.

ISBN 978-0-88754-837-6

1. Canadian drama (English)--Ontario. 2. Youths' writings, Canadian (English)--Ontario. 3. Canadian drama (English)--21st century.
I. Sokoloski, Robin

PS8315.5.O5U84 2008   C812'.60809283   C2008-904923-3

First edition: August 2008.
Printed and bound by Canadian Printco Ltd. at Scarborough, Canada.

Uth Ink's community and funding partners:

Myths & Mirrors
COMMUNITY ARTS

Great Canadian Theatre Company

THE ONTARIO
TRILLIUM
FOUNDATION

LA FONDATION
TRILLIUM
DE L'ONTARIO

Uth Ink acknowledges the support of the Ontario Arts Foundation,
Ministry of Education and the Ministry of Culture.

*This book is dedicated to
Uthinkers everywhere!*

Thank you

Like any anthology, this one owes its life to many people: Annie Gibson at Playwrights Canada Press instantly had the vision to back this idea from the moment I mentioned it to her. Amela Simic at Playwrights Guild of Canada provided me with the guidance and support to make U[th] Ink a reality. Gabe Sawhney and Shawn Micallef from [murmur], who have worked diligently on U[th] Ink and have shared their idea as a major point of inspiration to this program. The playwrights: Emil Sher, Eleanor Albanese, Shirley Barrie, Kathleen McDonnell and Marjorie Chan who conveyed the art of playwriting to the program's participants. The program's facilitators, Kristina Watt, Lila Cano, Lynn Fisher, Melissa McGrath and Tina Roy who nurtured the process. The six community organizations in U[th] Ink's five participating communities: Great Canadian Theatre Company, Creative Neighbourhoods, Community Arts and Heritage Education Project, Orillia and District Arts Council, Lakeshore Arts and Myths and Mirrors Community Arts.

I must also recognize the hard work and encouragement received from Gillian Hards, Gosia Kosciolek, Susan Nagy, Kathleen Burke, Sanjay Shahani, Jodi Armstrong, Nancy Burgoyne and Joe Morrow.

And lastly, thank you to the young writers (Uthinkers) who dedicated their time, energy and hearts into U[th] Ink.

—Robin Sokoloski

Table of Contents

Introduction to Uᵗʰ Ink: Word from the Street

When I was young I use to play a game with my best friend where we would run from one location to another. At every place we stopped, one of us had to recall a memory of something we had previously done there. Back then, we would most likely admit to playing this game out of sheer boredom. However, I would now boast that we did it because we were creative kids that identified with our community. This desire to discover identity through place is what most likely attracted me to the [murmur] program and inspired Uᵗʰ Ink.

September 2008 embarked Uᵗʰ Ink's first year of programming in five different communities throughout Ontario. Although I had organized youth art programs in the past, Uᵗʰ Ink involves many people who work in a variety of different ways. However, I was reassured by the one commonality that we all shared: Uᵗʰ Ink's philosophy.

The philosophy behind Uᵗʰ Ink is to give young people a voice in their community. Unfortunately, there are many gaps when mapping a community's perspective. Oftentimes, youth in the community are excluded from how one sees a city, town or neighbourhood. Uᵗʰ Ink offers an opportunity to give young people a chance to imprint their own identify upon the many layers of what makes that community unique.

When piecing the program together, one of the most vital elements was to identify community organizations that were not only willing to take a risk on delivering a multi-faceted first-year program, but also ones that genuinely support young voices. One of my greatest discoveries in creating and developing the Uᵗʰ Ink program was that there are many organizations in Canada that are youth arts driven. The potential that Uᵗʰ Ink has to help strengthen a network amongst its participating organizations gives me great pleasure.

U[th] Ink has many points of inspirations, one of which is the internationally acclaimed [murmur] program. [murmur] is an oral history documentary project created by Gabe Sawhney, Shawn Micallef and James Rousell that records stories and memories told about specific geographic locations. U[th] Ink applied the [murmur] mechanism, making U[th] Ink dynamic, current and relevant to a young person's culture.

U[th] Ink complies with [murmur]'s mandate by asking each young participant to select a particular physical location within their community and weave it into their own three-minute play. The plays that have been compiled in this anthology, interpret this piece of the program in a variety of ways. The initial intention was to use the physical location as the play's setting, however, some created imaginary worlds upon the actual space, others recounted historical facts, or their own personal memories about the location and then others simply translated how that particular location made them feel. Utilizing playwriting as a mode of artistic expression to interpret the young person's perspective allowed the young playwrights to explore different directions.

In addition, the professional playwrights and community facilitators that guided this course developed a "community within a community." This gave the participants a safe place to express themselves and experience new opportunities.

I am proud to say that the following plays are one hundred percent conceived and written by young playwrights. The Uth Ink program is designed, supported and delivered by the community that it has united. Yet, it is the young individuals (Uthinkers) that have breathed life into this program in such an outstanding way.

Therefore, I welcome you to journey through the Uth Ink community and its varying perspectives. I can promise you that you'll never look at these neighbourhoods the same way again.

Robin Sokoloski
U[th] Ink Program Manager

Uth Ink
Ottawa

Community Organizations
Creative Neighbourhoods
Great Canadian Theatre
Company

Playwright Facilitator
Emil Sher

Community Facilitator
Kristina Watt

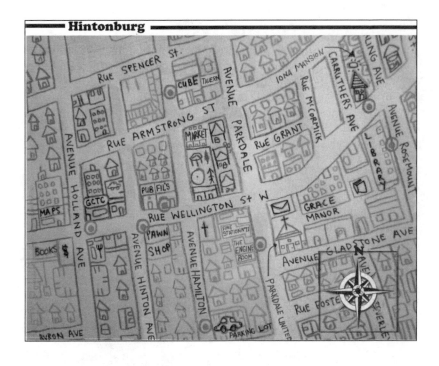

Each of the places marked with a dot on the map indicates a play's location.
Map illustrated by Trevor Sylvain

Where Does the Time Go?
Petra Smith

<u>Site-Specific Location</u>
Wellington Street West at Carruthers Avenue

An old woman drops her bag of groceries in front of a once elite building called Iona Mansions. Without hesitation, a young woman rushes to her aid.

JANNYN
Oh my goodness! Let me help you with those. Are you all right?

MARTHA
Oh yes, yes. Thank you dear. *(nostalgically)* You know, I remember the last time I dropped my groceries. It was actually right in front of this building. I used to live here, you know.

JANNYN
(in a hurried, insincere tone) Gee that's nice. Do you know where that orange rolled off to?

MARTHA
It's behind your foot. You know, when my husband and I lived here, we payed twenty-five dollars a month in rent. A very stately sum in the mid-forties. Could you manage to reach that can of tuna?

JANNYN
Of course. Just out of curiosity, what did you do to occupy your time during the days back then?

MARTHA
I was a working woman. Down at the Royal Bank. Stay loyal to the Royal, that's what I always say.

JANNYN
You mean that Royal Bank right there? *(gesturing west)*

MARTHA

Oh that new thing? Heavens no. It used to be the A&W when I worked at the bank. I took my kids there for a hamburger as a special treat every once in a while. When I had the money, that is. *(in a slightly concerned and miffed tone)* Those eggs are a lost cause, I'm afraid.

JANNYN

(excitedly) So where was the old bank?

MARTHA

It moved around quite a bit. When I worked there it was on Wellington and Fairmont. Mind those cabbages, dear.

JANNYN

Did you get those at the Parkdale Market?

MARTHA

Yes. On hot days like these I don't feel like going all the way to the Loebs. *(She pronounces it "Loebs" instead of "Loeb" because she's old and can't be bothered to learn the proper name.)* It was so much more convenient when the A&P was here.

JANNYN

Where was it?

MARTHA

On the corner of Wellington and Stirling. It actually used to be called Mr. Gilchrist's Groceries. Before they went out of business that is. Fine man, Mr. Gilchrist. Always giving my wee ones free sweeties.

JANNYN

Why did he go out of business?

MARTHA

You know, I'm not too sure. It was all right once the A&P was in though. They had two cash registers. Believe it or not, that was the talk of the town for a couple weeks. No stores, and I mean no stores, had two cash registers back then.

JANNYN

Oh my goodness! Look at the time!

MARTHA

I suppose you have things to do, people to see.

JANNYN

Yeah, I have to meet up with some friends at the Ethiopian restaurant.

MARTHA

Oh, I see. Young people these days, they eat all sorts of strange things.

JANNYN

What do you mean, strange?

MARTHA

I mean things they didn't have when I was growing up.

JANNYN

I think you should try it sometime, you might be surprised.

MARTHA

Surprises start to lose their appeal at my age.

JANNYN

I'm not so sure about that… *(hesitating)*

MARTHA

Martha, *(gesturing towards herself)* and you are?

JANNYN

Jannyn. But my friends call me JJ.

MARTHA

Well JJ, if you ever have the time, I suggest you diddle-daddy across the street and take a good long look at this building. If you look hard enough, you just might see the angel.

JANNYN

I promise I will if you promise to try Ethiopian food.

MARTHA

Not a chance, dear, not a chance. But I'm sure I'll see you again, though… right?

JANNYN

Of course.

MARTHA

Thank you for helping me with my groceries.

JANNYN

(her voice in the distance) No problem, bye!!

MARTHA

(muttering to herself) Oh, yes. Times are changing.

Rosemount Library
Emma Childs

<u>Site-Specific Location</u>

Rosemount Avenue at Wellington Street West

EMMA

Isn't it funny how an entire city can change, but some places just seem to stay the same? Rewind twelve years. *(sound of a tape rewinding)* I was only four and very curious for my age. A big adventure for me was taking a trip to the Rosemount Library. To me, the old building was filled with all sorts of adventures. Once inside the main doors, there were two ways to get to the bookshelves. You could take the stairs or the elevator. Every time that I visited the library with my mom, we would race. She would take the stairs and I would ride the elevator. The stairs were obviously the faster choice, but my mom always let me win. I would then head directly for the children's section and look for a book with exciting pictures. I remember my mom always trying to get me to read chapter books, but I always refused. I remember letting her check out a couple novels from *The Boxcar Children* series, but I never read them. I preferred books that made me imagin—like *Clifford the Big Red Dog*. I remember after being introduced to those books, I would always fantasize of owning a huge dog. How cool would that be? I preferred books like these because I could spend more time trying to live in the story than trying to understand the words.

Twelve years ago, the library was an intriguing place. I didn't care that it was then seventy-seven years old; its history didn't matter to me at all. All I cared about was the excitement of borrowing a book all for myself. Fast-forward three years. *(sound of a tape fast-forwarding)* I am seven years old and I discover the library in my school. There's no need to go all the way to Rosemount anymore. Why travel so far when I have another library so close? Besides, the only books I read now are the ones I need for book reports or school projects. Fast-forward another three years. *(sound of a tape fast-forwarding)* I am ten and haven't visited the library for a long time. I walk there and seem to take the same route I always used to. I remember whenever I reached the parking lot in front of the library I would take the shortcut and cross through it diagonally. As soon as I climb the stairs inside the doors, I notice the layout of the children's section is different. There are now more toys and puzzles laid out on tables for kids to play with. I stumble along the fiction aisles and only borrow a book if it really catches my eye. Five years later *(sound of a tape fast-forwarding)* I'm fifteen and I usually only use the library when I desperately need a book for school. I hate walking all the way there because I feel like there are so many other things I could be doing with my time. As a teenager, I am quite lazy. The books I borrow are usually for school, but occasionally I will borrow a popular book that my friends have been advising me to read, like *Gossip Girl* or the Georgia Nicolson series. I am grateful for the library, because buying books can get very costly. Today I am sixteen, *(sound of a tape fast-forwarding)* and I still haven't forgotten about my Rosemount memories. When I walk to the library, I still take the shortcut through the parking lot. I don't ride the elevator anymore, but I always give it a glance. It's been twelve years since I first started visiting the Rosemount library and I have changed a lot since then.

As people change over the years, it's important to have a place that will always stay the same for everyone. In some ways, I guess you could say the library has changed with society. The search engines on the computers are faster, there are now media resources and I can even request books online, from my home. But the thing about the library that will always stay the same is the purpose it continues to serve: it will always be the place for people to come together and share resources. In a world so fast-paced, it's nice to know that the library will stay on the corner of Wellington and Rosemount, like it has for eighty-nine years.

Cube Gallery
Emma Monet

Site-Specific Location
7 Hamilton Avenue North

EMMA

Quickly! Look down. What do you see?

I know, nothing interesting, just a bit of cement, maybe some grass. Wait, is that a penny? Nice shoes by the way! Keep looking down. Just imagine, millions of people have walked on this very spot for one reason or another, and this is one of them. Now look up: Taadaaa! You are looking at the Cube Gallery…. A modern art gallery.

The Cube is a hangout and meeting place for me and my friends. It belongs to my dad. He says I am a part owner— Mooohhhaaaaaa! Foolish mortal!

But this building wasn't always the Cube Gallery. Back in the days of the First World War it was an army barracks, then (during what my dad calls the Cold War) a factory for spy equipment and gizmos for jet planes. It had a weird name, Sperry Gyroscope…. After that it made the drastic change to Stubby Soda Pop factory! Can you imagine?

One year you see soldiers marching down the street and the next you see a bunch of kids lined up to get cases of grapefruit soda! Errghhhh—that's creepy! A soda pop factory in the same building that a bunch of guys with smelly socks who haven't showered recently used to sleep in!

But today it's an art gallery. Muuuch better!

Oh my gosh! I hear my dad throws great parties! People come from all over to talk, look at art and listen to music. Sometimes he has live music, catering and even dancers. I wouldn't know, I'm never invited.

Actually, I was invited to one party, except I was doing the inviting, my grade six graduation party. Look down the street towards the river…. Can you imagine seventy-six kids dressed up in grad clothes walking up the street towards you? We would never have made it as a squad of soldiers the way we kept laughing and fooling around!

These days I come to the Cube almost every night of the week.

Can I tell you a secret? A few of the paintings in my dad's gallery are actually done by me! Here's the way it works: whenever he has a show coming up, I leave a package of paintings at his front door with a fake name on it! I have many different styles and names. The more popular ones are Gerilda Manning Stephen. She does mostly sculptures of animals out of clay; then there is Johnny Clueman. He makes abstract paintings that incorporate different paint pastels and fabric. What do you call it? Oh yeah, mixed media! My most famous one is Jenny Turango. She does paintings of landscapes using melted crayon wax! She is awesome…. Dad really wants to meet her.

But, seriously, there are many other artists who show at the Cube too. Some of their names are Clare Brennan, Peggy Hughes and Russell Yuristy. Russell does both paintings and woodcuts, and you can even find some of his work in the National Gallery downtown!

Anyway, the Cube is definitely a place of history. Who knows what it will be next! Oh, and I actually really do like your shoes.

Community Within a Community
Megan Cowie

Site-Specific Location
Wellington Street West at Holland Avenue

ACTOR ONE
So, sis, where is this coffee shop you keep talking so much about?

ACTOR TWO
Is that on your mind all the time? Don't worry. We're getting closer.

ACTOR ONE
Hintonburg is quite quaint isn't it? Look at the nice little... pubs! Hey, that may help take the chill off.

ACTOR TWO
I thought you wanted coffee...

ACTOR ONE
I do. Hey, wasn't there a car wash there? I know it has been a while since I've been here but what is that building?

ACTOR TWO
It's a theatre now. The Great Canadian Theatre Company. Better known as the GCTC.

ACTOR ONE
Now that's an odd place for a theatre. It looks like it's part of an apartment building.

ACTOR TWO
This is not your regular kind of theatre.

ACTOR ONE
(interrupting) I keep thinking about that car wash. Remember how it was painted? An indescribable yellow.

ACTOR TWO

The car wash was replaced by a condo. The GCTC was looking for a new home and found it in Hintonburg. You don't often see a theatre and a condo together.

ACTOR ONE

I just thought it was a regular building. It almost looks different now…. You know what I mean?

ACTOR TWO

You wouldn't think they would have a theatre like this in Hintonburg. This community has the Cube Gallery just down the street on Hamilton, but it could be misleading because there aren't really a lot of places for the arts. But with the theatre being here it's a start of something shifting. I was lucky enough to see the first show at the GCTC main stage theatre, called *The Man from the Capital*. You could feel the excitement in the air!

ACTOR ONE

I'm going to have to experience this place for myself.

ACTOR TWO

Powerful theatre changes you. You know, with the theatre being in Hintonburg it's going to have an influence on the community. What better thing to do for an evening then to get together with a bunch of your family and friends to see another perspective, and be affected by that. Who knows, sis? Maybe you'll laugh like you've never laughed before.

ACTOR ONE

Or cry like you've never cried before.

ACTOR TWO

Yeah, or cry. You're giving and receiving. You pay a small fee to be changed, and the theatre continues to change the community.

ACTOR ONE

So what do you think this does for Hintonburg?

ACTOR TWO

I think Hintonburg and the GCTC have an opportunity to grow together. The theatre can help the community by offering plays and workshops to the public and the people of Hintonburg can support the theatre by making it a part of their community.

ACTOR ONE

With all this talk, I forgot one vital thing, coffee! What do you say we talk more over a cup of coffee?

ACTOR TWO

Coffee sounds great.

ACTOR ONE

Where are you going?

ACTOR TWO

Oh, did I forget to mention it? There's a restaurant in the theatre. We can grab a coffee there.

ACTOR ONE

Now that's a type of theatre I can get into.

Memories of a Parking Lot
Emianna Vargatoth

<u>Site-Specific Location</u>

Hamilton Avenue at Tyndall Street

> *POLLY is eight and EMIANNA is her older sister. POLLY wakes up EMIANNA at 7:30 a.m. on a Saturday.*

POLLY

Emi! Emi! Wake up!

EMIANNA

Polly, *(groan)* it's Saturday morning and… it's 7:30!

POLLY

I know, but you need to come outside with me, across the street to the parking lot.

EMIANNA

Can I at least get dressed?

POLLY

No, it's a surprise, you need to come now!

EMIANNA

Okay, okay, I'm coming!

POLLY

Here's your boots, let's go, close your eyes, I'll lead you.

Sound of boots running in the snow.

Okay, you can open your eyes, we're across the street.

EMIANNA

It's snowed! The first snow of the year!

POLLY

I love the parking lot in the winter. There's not a lot of snow, but when there's enough let's build snow forts.

EMIANNA

It's great the way the snow plough piles all the snow from the street on the sides of the parking lot. Remember a couple of years ago, when there wasn't very much snow but it was cold? We grabbed our skates and did some skating!

POLLY

That was soooo cool! And remember in the spring when all the snow had melted and I found a twenty dollar bill. Then I went through the alley to the Jaguar's corner store and bought all the neighbourhood kids Freezies?

EMIANNA

And in the summer when we took chalk and drew houses and roads on the pavement. It was like a real town because all the neighbourhood kids came here, and there were small families. Remember how we used our bicycles as cars, and we all had jobs.

POLLY

I was a police officer!

EMIANNA

Yeah and a tough one too!

POLLY

And in the fall when we raked all the leaves into a huge pile, then we jumped into it.

EMIANNA

All fun until you landed on me, and I had a bruise for a week.

POLLY

It was an accident, and plus, you should have looked where you landed! We almost spend more time in the parking lot than at our house, it is really too bad that we're not allowed here at night.

EMIANNA

It's for safety reasons, Polly, there have been some bad things here. Remember when the police arrested somebody in here?

POLLY

That was scary, but I thought it was interesting the way they broke down the door of the house backing on the alley.

EMIANNA

Polly, that was dangerous, there were drug dealers.

POLLY

Yeah, but it was the first time I had seen police actually break down a door! It was like a movie and we were actors in it!

EMIANNA

Oh, Polly, you're hopeless, you don't know the difference between life and fantasy. But I do wish it would be considerably cleaned up. Then maybe we could have a street party here at night. It might be cool! But we were really lucky when we moved here in 2000, that it was across the street. Did you know that three houses burnt down here, before we moved?

POLLY

Really?

EMIANNA

Yeah, it's true, Dad told me, that's why it's even here. After the houses burnt down the Baptist church bought it and paved it. It's great the way there are only cars here on Sundays.

POLLY

That's sad for the people who used to live there, but good for us!

EMIANNA

Yep! It's really great for the whole neighbourhood. Not just the kids, parents are here sometimes with their kids to play basketball and other games.

POLLY

Well, yeah, it's a big empty open space that's hardly ever full of cars. Why not take advantage of it?

EMIANNA

This parking lot holds memories, good, bad, happy, sad. *(pause)*

More Than Just a Diner
Shannon Bain

<u>Site-Specific Location</u>
Wellington Street West at Hamilton Avenue

SOPHIA
Hello, Amelia. How are you today?

AMELIA
Fine, fine, and yourself, Sophia?

SOPHIA
Fine, I suppose. My back's been acting up a little lately, but it's fine now.

AMELIA
The usual I'm guessing then?

SOPHIA
Oh no! I'm going to try something new. Ummm.... How's about the soup of the day?

AMELIA
Tomato? Don't you always have tomato soup?

SOPHIA
Yes, but it's never been the soup of the day. I'll have a tea as well.

AMELIA
All right.... A tomato soup and some tea. I'll be back.

SOPHIA
Thanks Amelia, and take your time, I have all morning. And all afternoon, to think of it. Ouch! Now where did I put my needles? Hmm... not under there.... Excuse me sir, have you seen my knitting needles? No? That's fine. Oh! There they are! Ouch! They're sharp!

AMELIA

Here's your soup. The tea's brewing. Who are you knitting that scarf for? Charlie?

SOPHIA

No, no, his wife. They live all the way out in Vancouver, and you know how the winters are there.

AMELIA

Oh, well, that's nice. Tell your son I said hi. I'll go get your tea now.

SOPHIA

Right! And some little tea biscuits too! Hmm…. It looks cold out. I'm glad I'm inside with the heat.

AMELIA

Careful, it's hot.

SOPHIA

Thank you, Amelia. So, I heard that some big-time corporation wanted to buy the land and make it into a parking lot. The thing is… if they sell it, I don't know what I'd do. The old *I Love Lucy* posters and the old Coca-Cola commercials make me feel like I'm back in my childhood.

AMELIA

Yeah, out of all my jobs, I do like this one the best. The owners make me feel very at home. If they sold it, I'd lose a big part of my life.

SOPHIA

I just wish you'd stop playing the Elvis music over and over again.

AMELIA

(*chuckles*) It seems like you've been coming here forever. How long have you been coming anyway?

SOPHIA

Oh! Since it opened in 2000…

AMELIA

Why do you like it so much?

SOPHIA

Well, ever since my husband died I've been very lonely, and Fil's Diner is just up the road, and you and the other waitresses make me feel very at home.

AMELIA

Well, remember, you're always welcome here…. If it stays, that is.

SOPHIA

Thanks. *(pause)* My tea doesn't have any biscuits beside it.

AMELIA

Oh! Sorry. I'll go get them…

SOPHIA

Take your time… I've got all day.

Pawnshop
Andrew Woodhead

Site-Specific Location

Hinton Avenue at Wellington Street West

CUSTOMER is looking for gold, but is being very unhelpful with her explanation while PAWNSHOP OWNER is getting more and more frustrated.

PAWNSHOP OWNER is whistling when the old woman enters.

PAWNSHOP OWNER
Good day, ma'am, how are you this morning?

CUSTOMER
Oh, well I am good, but I am looking for some gold to make me look flashier. I heard this pawnshop sells some nice gold.

PAWNSHOP OWNER
Gold eh? We have a lot of gold for you to choose from, we have gold with jewels that you might like.

CUSTOMER
Yes, well that is very nice, but I don't think you get it. I need some gold that is very flashy. I need to impress all the gentlemen at the church down the road, so I need some flashy gold.

PAWNSHOP OWNER
No, I gotcha, ma'am, I was just trying to say that…

CUSTOMER
No, I think we need to look at your gold because I need to look flashy.

PAWNSHOP OWNER
Okay, ma'am, right this way.

CUSTOMER
Where are you taking me?

PAWNSHOP OWNER
To look at the gold.

CUSTOMER
No…. But I want to look at the gold. You young kids never listen…. So, dear, can you show me the gold.

PAWNSHOP OWNER
I got it, ma'am, but it is on this table.

CUSTOMER
Yes, but I am trying to look flashy. I don't want your smelly green gold, I want your flashy gold. Show me your gold, okay?

PAWNSHOP OWNER
Right over here.

CUSTOMER
Okay. How long have you owned this shop?

PAWNSHOP OWNER
Oh, I've owned this for the last couple of years; it is an easy business to keep goin', so, you know. I've actually lived here since I was a kid and I decided I wanted to raise my family here as well. Umm, why don't you take a look at this one?

CUSTOMER
Oh, this one is nice, but it makes me look like a hussy, don't you think?

PAWNSHOP OWNER
No, it makes you look really nice, ma'am.

CUSTOMER
That's just because you like hussies.

PAWNSHOP OWNER
No, ma'am, I don't like…

CUSTOMER
Oooo, look at this. It is sooo pretty. Let me try it on.

PAWNSHOP OWNER

I don't like huss…. Yes, ma'am. Do you live in the neighbour-hood?

CUSTOMER

Oh, I've been here for the last couple of decades, hon. I bought my house when that there church down the road was a movie theatre. I lived right at the top of Hamilton. So, what do you think? Is it flashy enough?

PAWNSHOP OWNER

It's pretty nice.

CUSTOMER

Oh, you are just saying that.

PAWNSHOP OWNER

No, miss, it really looks good.

CUSTOMER

You're just lying to me. I don't want it. It isn't flashy enough. Lemme see that one. That is cute. It looks like something Marilyn Monroe would wear, don'tcha think?

PAWNSHOP OWNER

Actually, that is a replica of a Marilyn Mon…

CUSTOMER

Hush now, I think I want it.

PAWNSHOP OWNER

Yes, ma'am. Let's bring it to the cash.

CUSTOMER

Yeah, okay, but you gotta hurry up there.

PAWNSHOP OWNER

Yes ma'am. Do you have any children in the area?

CUSTOMER

Of course, dear. I have two sons that live on Hinton Avenue who have their children attending Fisher Park. They are so sweet. I'm buying this gold for their communion at the church down the road. Do you have any kids?

PAWNSHOP OWNER
No, ma'am, not yet. I have thought of having my kids here as well, but I find that once you live here, you just don't want to leave.

CUSTOMER
That is true, especially with all these new building projects that have been popping up; this has become quite the hip neighbourhood. Can you ring that through, dear, price really isn't an issue, so don't you worry about that.

PAWNSHOP OWNER
I won't, ma'am.

CUSTOMER
So, you just tell me the price and I will pay, okay?

PAWNSHOP OWNER
Okay, ma'am, it will be about fifty-seven dollars.

CUSTOMER
No, I don't think you did the math right. That is too much for this.

PAWNSHOP OWNER
No, I did the math…

CUSTOMER
No no no, that's not right, you just go and do it again, okay?

PAWNSHOP OWNER
Okay, ma'am, but it isn't going to change anything.

CUSTOMER
You just pipe down and do the math, okay. It is too expensive, you know?

PAWNSHOP OWNER
Yes, ma'am. No, the math is all right, fifty-seven dollars flat.

CUSTOMER
Well, that is just ridiculous. I can't believe you. You are trying to take advantage of a little old lady like me. You are so rude, you know. That is really low, you know.

PAWNSHOP OWNER

Ma'am, it is fifty-seven dollars. Whether you buy it or not isn't my problem.

CUSTOMER

Why are you trying to scam me, I'm old can't you see? I'm *old*!

PAWNSHOP OWNER

Ma'am, please don't speak to me like that.

CUSTOMER

I'm going. You know, that isn't the way to sell your things. You remember that, okay? You remember that.

PAWNSHOP OWNER

I hope you enjoy your grandchildrens' communion, ma'am.

CUSTOMER

Thank you. Goodbye. Hmph!

430 Parkdale/The Engine Room
Acacia Frojmovic

Site-Specific Location
430 Parkdale Avenue

Contemporary music plays in the background.

STEPHEN
Hey, Raymond?

RAYMOND
Yes?

STEPHEN
Before we officially shut down Berrigan's Repair Garage, can
we take a moment to talk about some of our memories here at
430 Parkdale?

RAYMOND
How about the one when you and I found the old photo in the
garage behind the house?

STEPHEN
Sounds good to me!

RAYMOND
You were nine and I was twelve, years before we took over the
Repair Garage from Dad. It went something like this...

Early 1960s music plays in the background.

STEPHEN
Hey, Ray! What's this?

RAYMOND
What's the problem now? Can't you see I'm working on my
new car? I tell you, I'm so good at these models, I think I'll own
a repair shop someday, just like Dad.

STEPHEN

(sigh) Okay. That's nice, but do you think you could spare just two minutes? I think I've found something!

RAYMOND

Hey, that looks like an old photo stuck behind the car hoist.

STEPHEN

Let's go get it!

RAYMOND

No! Dad told us to never touch the hoists.

STEPHEN

Why? Why don't you ever want to do anything fun with me? You're so boring! *(pauses, thinking RAYMOND will say something back)* Well, fine! If you're going to ignore me, I'll ask Dad to help!

RAYMOND

Steve, no. Dad's busy! He's in the middle of fixing a customer's car!

MR. BERRIGAN

Boys! You're not fighting again are you?

STEPHEN & RAYMOND

(innocently) No!

MR. BERRIGAN

Well, then what was all that commotion? I could hear you two shouting even with my machinery on.

STEPHEN

Well, Raymond didn't want to...

RAYMOND

What Stephen means to say is that I didn't want to bother you. It's just that we found a photo stuck behind the hoist and we were really excited.

MR. BERRIGAN

Wow! I haven't seen this picture in years! Why, the last time

I saw it would have to have been about ten years ago, when I first opened the garage.

RAYMOND
Where was this picture taken?

MR. BERRIGAN
Well, it's right here! It's a photo of the old Hibernia Dance Hall. In fact, where you two are standing is right around where the band would play every Friday night.

STEPHEN
It must have been a really small dance hall.

MR. BERRIGAN
Why do you say that, Stephen?

STEPHEN
Well, if it was only as big as this garage...

MR. BERRIGAN
No, silly, the Hibernia Dance Hall used to take up the whole property until it burnt down sometime during the Depression. Kind of a strange thing when you realize the fire station was right beside it!

STEPHEN
Oh, that's too bad.

RAYMOND
Was there anything else here before the dance hall, Dad?

MR. BERRIGAN
Come to think of it, there was. Some of the older neighbours told me that years before the Dance Hall opened, the building was the Hintonburg Town Hall. I'm actually not quite so sure why it was turned into a dance hall though...

RAYMOND
Hey, Dad, there's someone at the door for you.

MR. BERRIGAN
Oh, of course, boys, I nearly forgot. I'm expecting an important customer.

STEPHEN

Do you have to talk to him now? Why can't you play with me?

MR. BERRIGAN

Sorry, I'd love to spend more time with you two, but business is business.

Contemporary music plays in the background.

STEPHEN

To think, that a dance hall would have been standing here during the Depression. Even in a time like that, people still found space in their lives to go dancing! I guess they needed something to keep their spirits up.

RAYMOND

Speaking of spirits, I'm really going to miss being around here. We made so many good friends running the neighbourhood garage.

STEPHEN

Hey, do you know what they'll be doing with the whole space?

RAYMOND

They probably won't continue the repair shop…. I believe it'll be some kind of artists' space. They're going to call it The Engine Room. They'll rent it out to sculptors or even designers. The parking lot will be a courtyard—it'll be a nice change from our greasy garage and pothole-filled lot!

STEPHEN

What about the house?

RAYMOND

I imagine it will still be a residence. They will either live in it or rent it out.

STEPHEN

(*sadly*) Sounds like all in all, this will be a really nice property.

RAYMOND

Why the sad tone?

STEPHEN

I guess hearing all the great things the family is going to do to this place, just makes me miss it even more.

RAYMOND

I'm going to miss it, too. It seems like we're leaving just as this neighbourhood is really changing. For goodness sake, there's even going to be a theatre and some kind of green building around the corner!

STEPHEN

How about a toast to our departure—to memories of the past!

RAYMOND

Wait! Don't think of it as the past and the end. Just because we're leaving doesn't mean the property is finished. I think our toast should be to the future.

STEPHEN

You're right. To the future?

STEPHEN & RAYMOND

To the future!

Uᵗʰ Ink
Thunder
Bay

**Community
Organizations**
Community Arts and Heritage
Education Project

**Playwright and
Community Facilitator**
Eleanor Albanese

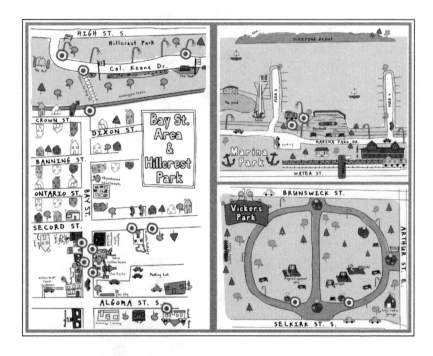

Each of the places marked with a dot on the map indicates a play's location.
Map illustrated by Alana Forslund

Natural Beauty
Christopher Brown

Site-Specific Location
Hillcrest Park by the stairs that lead to Bay Street

CHRIS

I was out with my family and we had just finished dinner with
our cousins. As we were driving home, my mother was telling
us how nice the sky was as we were making the drive up High
Street off Oliver Road. She then made the suggestion of stopping at Hillcrest Park to finish the night with some star gazing.
I will never forget the look on my little cousin's faces when they
ran to the hill's ledge overlooking the city and all they could
say was "Wow!" It was silent for only a brief second before my
whole family lit up in conversation of all the observations they
made. I was speechless. This was my first real experience with
this place. It was something that could have stolen your heart.
Looking over the city lights, each one was adjacent to a star in
the sky, creating an almost common characteristic between
heaven and earth. Walking down the stairs is almost the same
as descending from a dream world. With each step you take
down the hill, which connects to Bay Street, you lose a little
piece of the power that you feel on top of the hill. That's why I
love it up on the hill. Sunrise, noon and sunset, it's beautiful.
There isn't anything you can't see! Not many people can say
they have experienced Thunder Bay beauty, natural beauty.
That's what it comes down to; it is a naturally beautiful city. I
would never take a night in an elaborate city, with all the pleas-
ures a man or woman could want, over one night under the
Thunder Bay sky, up here, on this hill. But, if there is one thing
that I can say I now have a better understanding for, it is this
quote by Dag Hammarskjold. "Never look down to test the
ground before taking your next step. Only they who keep their
eyes fixed on the far horizon will find the right road." So take a
good look at the sky, you never know what you might see.

Surprises in Reality
Philip Duke

Site-Specific Location
Hoito restaurant, 314 Bay Street

PHILIP

I opened my case before eight this morning. Sitting on this concrete ledge, looking at the people lining up for Hoito pancakes and big breakfasts. On the weekends, people line up even before it opens. It's a good spot to play my violin.

The sound of a fiddle playing. The sound of coins dropping into the violin case.

Thanks!

PERSON

Nice playing.

PHILIP

What would you like to hear next? A jig or a reel? Maybe a waltz?

PERSON

Your choice. It all sounds good to me.

A few more bars of music are played.

VIOLIN-MAKER

Ho there. Pretty chilly day to be out here playing.

PHILIP

That's okay. It's warming up now. Later, it gets too hot.

VIOLIN-MAKER

Once that sun comes out. Not much shade out here. How long you been playing?

PHILIP

At the moment, I've been fiddling five years.

VIOLIN-MAKER
Do you play with that group, Kam Valley Fiddlers?

PHILIP
Actually, yeah, I do.

VIOLIN-MAKER
I play violin, too. I used to play a lot more when I was younger, like you.

PHILIP
Really?

VIOLIN-MAKER
I make violins, too. For more than thirty years I've made violins. Mind if I play a tune?

PHILIP
Ahhhh… shshsh-sure. Why not?

The VIOLIN-MAKER plays a song with a Hungarian sound.

Wow. That's cool.

VIOLIN-MAKER
Back to you!

PHILIP
After the stranger walked back into the Finlandia club, I started noticing things I never noticed before, like the words carved into the walls in big block letters. On one side, it reads "LABOR" and on the other side it's "VINCIT." I'll have to ask someone what "vincit" means. In the middle, on the turret-window tower way at the top of the building, it reads "OMNIA 1910." I guess that's when this place was built.

Beyond
Hanna Dorval

Site-Specific Location
Marina Park, north of the parking lot

HANNA

Standing outside in the cold, it is hard to imagine that it will ever be summer again. But whenever I look out towards the Sleeping Giant, all sorts of warm, fun, summer memories flood back to me. Looking out from where you are standing, you see Lake Superior, and the large cliffs and rocks that we know as the Sleeping Giant. But when I look out, I see a shield, a guard, who watches over a big piece of my heart, Silver Islet. Even though I can't see Silver Islet from where I stand, I always know that it is there, and it has been since long before I was born, which means it is pretty old. And it has a lot of history, such as the fact that it used to be the world's richest silver mine in the late 1800s. There are many stories about Silver Islet. But there's also some history that my friends and I have created out at my camp as well.

My friends and I have seen the best northern lights ever, that were green, vibrant and danced for us all night long. We also do things like make watermelon boats, which glow like hot pink lily pads once it gets dark out, and we can make golden, floating balloons. We start with McDonald's straws, which we simply tape together to form a cross. We put small slits along the straws, and in each slit we place a tiny birthday candle. We tightly tape a dry cleaner bag over the lit candles, creating a sort of billowy case for all the hot air. Once we let it go on the lake, it flies off into the winter night and we watch it drift away into the distance until it becomes a tiny golden star among the other millions of stars in the sky. Where else can you make magic like that?

Train Treats
Alexis Hell

<u>Site-Specific Location</u>

Marina Park

ALEXIS

Standing here, I'm thinking about how this old building used to
be a train station. Now it's a bunch of shops and restaurants.
There used to be an ice cream shop here that my papa used to
take me to in the summer. I'd spend hours just staring at the
miniature train that rode on the walls.

Papa, are there actual people in that train?

PAPA

Yes, little wooden people. And they drive it all day long, round
and round and round the room. But they never get dizzy!

ALEXIS

I wish I could drive a train.

PAPA

Only thing is, the real train doesn't run around here anymore,
not since the Mulroney government. A whole bunch of us went
out to the Syndicate station to watch the last passenger train.
Some people were mad as heck over that. But there's still trains
in other places. And Lexi driving a train? I like that idea.

ALEXIS

Me too, Papa.

PAPA

So, Lexi, what are we having today?

ALEXIS

Chocolate chip cookie dough. Papa, how'd they get the train up
on the roof like that?

PAPA

Well, a couple of guys climbed up a tall ladder and bolted the tracks to the wall. Or maybe the train drove itself up there. What do you think?

ALEXIS

I think they used a ladder.

PAPA

After ice cream, want to go to the playground?

ALEXIS

Can we come back though?

PAPA

We can come back until we try every flavour.

ALEXIS

But you always get the same kind.

PAPA

I better get busy then.

A Second Look
Thea Books

Site-Specific Location

Kivela Bakery, 109 Secord Street

THEA

I'm walking beside the Kivela bakery and I see this small base-
ment window with a small tree. And the window is cracked
because the branches of the tree are actually growing inside the
building. I wonder if anyone even knows that it's there. Do the
people who work at the bakery know about it? Maybe they do,
maybe its limbs are winding their way along the floorboards—
with apples on the branches——big, red, juicy, ready to be
picked.

But when I walk into the bakery, I realize I've just been carried
away with my imagination. Inside, I feel so warm and safe and
the smells of cardamon and yeast fill my lungs. Part of the wall
is covered in old wallpaper and the wallpaper has been made to
look like a mountain landscape, maybe the Rockies or
Appalachians. To the left and in front of me the bakery walls
are covered in old wood panelling, something from the seventies. Behind the sink in the back room there is old laminate
flooring that is peeling off. It looks like something once again
from the seventies with its burnt oranges and yellows. On the
counters, instead of baked goods, are piles of puzzles, it looks
like more than two dozen of them. Beside the sink is another
crossword puzzle—this one looks like a fall landscape.

When I ask about the puzzles, the baker, Mike, simply tells me
that he likes doing them. A few more people have come into the
shop. Mike asks us if we want to see the ovens where he does
all his baking. We all say yes and walk into the back room. The
smell of the spices gets stronger and we all take in deep breaths.
The oven is huge and warm, and it's nice to feel its warmth
after being outside in the mean winter weather. The inside of

the oven, which, by the way, is called baker boy, is very large and cavernous. When I look into it I feel the warmth, but something about its size and the flames in it make me feel a bit scared, too. It could probably hold hundreds of loaves, but there are only three long loaves. But they're good loaves—rye loaves that he bakes for the Hoito.

I step outside and look down at the little window again. I will never walk by an old building and not take a second look—like I did today.

Age Before Beauty
Emma Rapley

Site-Specific Location
Hillcrest Park by the bell

The scene begins with TAYLOR, who is lost. Sounds of her rustling through her purse and sounds of frustration as she can't find the piece of paper she's looking for.

TAYLOR
(to herself) Don't really want to talk to that person but... *(more rustling)* Excuse me. I'm.... Do you know where we are? I mean, I know this is Thunder Bay, but what's this place?

LINDA
I'm not sure what you mean.

TAYLOR
This park, I guess.

LINDA
Ohhhh. Hillcrest Park. Are you lost, dear?

TAYLOR
I don't know. I'm not lost. I'm just not sure exactly where I am.

LINDA
Well, you're at the Port Arthur end of the city. Are you trying to get somewhere?

TAYLOR
No, I'm just, you know, looking at the view. *(pause)* Yeah, I'm lost.

LINDA
Where were you last?

TAYLOR
Trying to get away from my obnoxious little cousin. Anyway,

I remember walking by this bright yellow house and some old church.

LINDA

With the wooden tower reaching up?

TAYLOR

Yeah, I think so.

LINDA

Is it that church down there? It's actually been turned into apartments.

TAYLOR

Right! That's the place I walked by. But...

LINDA

But what?

TAYLOR

It still doesn't help me find my auntie's house.

LINDA

Do you have your aunt's phone number? You could use my cell phone.

TAYLOR

I did. But—it's not in my purse. Okay, I think I remember the name of the street. It's on the tip of my tongue. Something about a queen or a tiara?

LINDA

Crown?

TAYLOR

That's it!

LINDA

Well, that's easy. Do you think you'd recognize the house?

TAYLOR

Of course. For sure.

LINDA

All you do is walk down here. Turn right as soon as you get to the bottom of the steps and that's Crown Street.

TAYLOR
Right there?

LINDA
Yeah, that's Crown.

TAYLOR
Thanks. Well, okay, bye.

LINDA
I hope you have a nice visit here.

TAYLOR
Well, I didn't really like Thunder Bay when I got here but I guess it's… what is it? Well, it's got nice people—except for my annoying cousin.

LINDA
I hope you do some more exploring. It really is full of some funny little quirks.

TAYLOR
I will. Bye.

LINDA
Bye.

Footprints in the Snow
Nadia Cheechoo

<u>Site-Specific Location</u>

Vickers Park

NADIA

Flashbacks of buried memories surface again. Old time
rememberances of me and my far-away friend.
Memories scattered all over, here and there.
There's no ground we haven't covered we've been everywhere.

I remember the time under the tree. She and I escaped the hot
rays from the sun in the blue sky. We noticed the couple across
the street. We've seen them before, but today was different.
Their voices didn't reach our curious ears, but their gestures
made it clear what was going on. This certain day there was no
hugging, no small pecks, only distance. Finally, the girl started
down the street. She did not look back, but he watched her
walk away. He sat on the steps outside his front door. His hands
in his hair, his face looking down. By then she was gone.

Everything seemed quiet the whole time it was happening. The
city noises came rushing back when it was through. The wind
rustled the green leaves above us as the sun peeked through the
tree.

I looked to the familiar face sitting beside me. A smile grew on
our faces. "Big loser," she teased, and laughter soared through
the air. We were continuing our day of smiles while they started
their day of frowns.

There are footprints pressed in the snow, they are lightly
covered with freshly fallen snowflakes. Sleeping trees surround
me, waiting until spring to awake.

Worn Paths
Eden Wilkins

Site-Specific Location
Vickers Park

EDEN

Since the last time I visited, the park is looking fairly dull. It's a feeling like it's been left by itself for the winter, hibernating. Lots of paths of those who've walked through this park are left behind. It's like memories are stored in the paths and new paths are being made all the time by couples, people walking alone, even dogs walking through the untouched snow. It seems like it was yesterday that I was here. It was spring and I was chasing two little kids. We were weaving through the trees and then we took a more obscure route. We ran about two or three laps around the entire park, and let me tell you, it was exhausting. After that we just laid in the grass watching the clouds. Today it's so empty. There are no children playing on the playground, no laughing, no one having picnics under the trees. There's barely any sounds. Only the odd bird and the sounds of cars racing behind me. Today it's so cold sitting here on the bench. No one around but a sturdy old lady wearing a long coat and a fur hat. And her poodle.

What a cute dog.

OLD WOMAN

She's very friendly.

EDEN

She's pretty excited about the snow.

OLD WOMAN

Oh, yes, she loves the snow all right. What a smart girl you are, coming out here in the winter so no one can bother you. It really is a nice idea.

She walks away.

EDEN

Now my footprints are left in the snow, carrying my story. It will be there forever.

Cookies and Puzzles
Georgia Wilkins

<u>   Site-Specific Location</u>
Kivela Bakery, 109 Secord Street

MICHAEL
Hello!

GEORGIA
Hi.

MICHAEL
Cold enough for you?

GEORGIA
It's nice and warm in here.

MICHAEL
It's all coming from the oven. Keeps me warm all day.

GEORGIA
What puzzle are you working on today?

MICHAEL
The Eiffel Tower. For the fifth time. So, two loaves of pula bread?

GEORGIA
No, I'm changing it up today.

MICHAEL
What'll it be then?

GEORGIA
A dozen cookies.

MICHAEL
Cookies! What's the event?

GEORGIA
My cousin just had twins.

MICHAEL

That'll be two dollars and fifty cents for a baker's dozen.

GEORGIA

Oh, sorry! I just remembered. I have to run to Bay Credit to get some cash.

MICHAEL

You know what used to be on that exact spot? The Bay Credit Union?

GEORGIA

Maybe a restaurant or shop?

MICHAEL

Close. It was the Algoma Steam Bath. I have an old photograph. Hang on, I'll show you. Not every town had a steam bath.

GEORGIA

I know. It's because of the Finns. They love saunas.

MICHAEL

Well now, it's cold today. How about I save you a trip and you just pay up next time?

GEORGIA

Thanks!

MICHAEL

And say hello to those new twins.

GEORGIA

I will.

Sound of a bell as the door opens and closes.

Five Cent Coffee
April O'Gorman and Thea Books

<u>Site-Specific Location</u>
Scandinavian Home restaurant, 147 Algoma Street South

THEA
Did you bring your nickel?

APRIL
No. Sorry.

THEA
I told you.

APRIL
But our moms will buy us pancakes. They always do.

THEA
Yes, but I was going to get something from the old big menu.

APRIL
Where?

THEA
On the stairs. You know, when we go to the bathroom. See? There's the big one.

APRIL
Look! The pancakes are only twenty-five cents.

THEA
Coffee is five cents.

APRIL
But we can't drink coffee. And I forgot my quarter, too.

THEA
It's okay.

APRIL

Want to see something neat? There's horses and dollies. It's all underneath the coats in the closet.

THEA

Mmmm. I'm too old for that. Let's just sit with our moms. Menu plan destructed.

Sound of kazoos to represent mothers talking.

You can sit beside your mom and I'll sit beside mine and then we can talk under the table.

More kazoo sounds.

APRIL

See my new monkey?

THEA

What's his name?

APRIL

Her name. It's Nellie McNellie.

THEA

Is she a zombie monkey?

APRIL

I don't know.

THEA

Well you have to put her in the freezer and see if her eyes get all frosty.

I have more whipped cream than you.

APRIL

Yeah, well, I'll just dip my strawberries in your whipped cream.

THEA

Well, I'll eat some of your strawberries.

More kazoo sounds.

APRIL

Did you know I have to move?

THEA
When?

APRIL
I don't know. I have to go to a new school and everything.

THEA
Are we still going to come here?

APRIL
I don't know if my mom can take me anymore.

THEA
My mom will take you. Okay?

APRIL
Okay.

Disappearing Giant
Devon Multimaki

<u>   **Site-Specific Location**</u>
Hillcrest Park by the tank

DEVON

It's icy and snowy. It's hard to feel anything but cold today. The Sleeping Giant is hidden behind the fog. It looks really cool. It's as if the Giant has disappeared.

I remember whenever my nana came to town; she always wanted to go to Hillcrest Park to see the view of the Giant. Something they don't have in big cities like Toronto. When I was young I used to be able to slip in between the bars of the cage where they keep the war tank. I climbed up onto the tank. I noticed the metal wasn't that strong. It aroused a bit of suspicion in me so I looked inside the window and I couldn't see anything in there. The tank was empty.

I can't remember if it was my sister who was there who said, "Check the gun on top." As I started to climb up on top I couldn't help but feel a bit restrained. I wanted to save myself the disappointment of finding out that the gun might be fake. I would rather believe that it was all real and better to leave my theory unconfirmed. I can't remember how old I was or how many times I climbed in there.

Funny how the Sleeping Giant is lost in fog today, just like my memories are partly in the back of my head.

First Memory
Conner McMahon

Site-Specific Location
Bay Street at Crown Street

CONNER

I was only a five-year-old boy when I gazed up into the sky
with my brother by my side, only to see an airplane plummet
into the calm surface of the harbour. The plane was a provincial
firefighter and the pilot was second in command in the forestry
service. He developed regulations against stunting. I had a clear
view of the accident from the comfort of our Crown Street yard.
The plane had betrayed its pilot by stalling in the midst of a
dazzling looping stunt. It was 1929. It's strange because later
on, on the very same day, my brother and I were watching an
elaborate funeral procession from the front steps of our home
on Crown Street. It was a massive walking procession of five
thousand people moving up Oliver Road, with many people
carrying large red flags. Many communist supporters were
there. The funeral was for two Finnish bush workers who were
organizing unions. The two workers had disappeared the previ-
ous fall and weren't found until that spring. The newspapers
reported that they had fallen through the ice. But of course,
many, many people did not believe their deaths were acciden-
tal. And if that didn't make the day strange enough, there was
one other event, an eclipse of the sun. At the time all these
events were connected in my five-year-old mind: the funeral,
the plane crash and the eclipse. I somehow thought the funeral
was for the pilot but it was actually for an entirely different reason. Isn't it strange how for months and months nothing
notable happens, and then three events happen on the same
day?

Latte Rings a Bell
Katie Robinson

<u>   Site-Specific Location</u>
Calico Coffee House, 316 Bay Street

GIRL ONE
How do we always end up here?

GIRL TWO
Because Nutty Irish Lattes take away the pain.

GIRL ONE
No, I mean "here," as in boyfriendless.

GIRL TWO
Oh, that. If I knew, I would still be here, but it wouldn't be with you, it would be with my boyfriend. No offence.

GIRL ONE
Yeah, well, I always had to pay for everything. Boyfriends are expensive.

GIRL TWO
Only your boyfriend.

GIRL ONE
Not just mine!

GIRL TWO
You just said you had to pay for stuff.

GIRL ONE
Yeah, well, he has a car. Your boyfriend doesn't have a car.

GIRL TWO
'Kay, let's stop talking about our boyfriends since we don't actually have boyfriends anymore.

GIRL ONE
'Kay.

Silence. Sound of girls slurping on their drinks.

So, do you have that assignment done? The one for writer's craft?

GIRL TWO
Kind of…. No, not really.

GIRL ONE
I'm not done either.

More sounds of slurping. GIRL ONE's cell phone rings.

Hi…. Nothing…. Sure…. 'Kay…. Calico…. 'Kay, bye.

GIRL TWO
Who was that?

GIRL ONE
Nothing. Oh, but I've gotta go in a couple minutes.

GIRL TWO
Where you going?

GIRL ONE
Dave's picking me up.

GIRL TWO
Are you kidding me? I thought you guys broke up.

GIRL ONE
We did. We're just friends now. 'Kay, bye.

GIRL TWO
Whatever. Bye.

Hidden Nest
Casey Sellers

Site-Specific Location
314 Bay Street

CASEY

Once upon a time did a barren tree occupy the winter drab
of Bay Street. Its bland and unimpressive appearance anti-daz-
zling all who gazed upon it. Then! A small birch bark bird's
nest, the glory of this sight makes me want to shrink down to
the size of a bird and make my way inside this tiny birch oasis.
I wonder, do the hundreds of people who carelessly stroll by
tossing their cigarette butts or gum wrappers ever stop to gaze
upon this last bastion of sanity in this sometimes bleak world?
Do they see the significance of the bird's nest? As I gaze up to
the window of the Finlandia Club, I don't believe they do. Their
apathy drifts out onto the street where I stand. My eyes begin to
tear. Who am I?

Down the Steps
Katie Robinson and Casey Sellers

<u>Site-Specific Location</u>

Harry's Pool Hall, 318 Bay Street

ANNIE

My eyes caught on an open door that I'd never seen before just beside Calico. There was a set of steps leading down into the unknown. I didn't have a clue what could be down there. And if my grandpa hadn't been with me, I just would've thought it was an old abandoned space. When I stepped past the door, it was cold and damp and dusty, but for some reason it fascinated me.

Grandpa? Grandpa, why's this door open?

GRANDPA

Ummm? What? What door?

ANNIE

This one right here. It's the middle of January.

GRANDPA

It's open every day. Monday to Sunday. Or Sunday to Sunday you could say.

ANNIE

Or Tuesday to Tuesday. So, what is down the dark steps?

GRANDPA

No, you're too young. I'm not giving you cigarettes.

ANNIE

No, I said dark steps.... Not cigarettes.

GRANDPA

Ohhhh! All sorts of cute boys are down there.

ANNIE

Grandpa...

GRANDPA

With bulging triceps.

ANNIE

Don't say that. You probably don't even know.

GRANDPA

Oh, I know all about this place. It opened up in, probably, just guessing, well, I came home from the war in…. So that means this pool hall's been here since, oh maybe '44, let's say. But then, the building's much older than that.

ANNIE

So it's a pool hall? Let's go down there.

GRANDPA

'24, that's when it opened. 1924! Or was it '25?

ANNIE

So, are you sure it's open?

GRANDPA

Oh yes, oh yes. Same snooker pool tables. Not those puny ones you see in the beer parlours today.

ANNIE

Beer parlours? Come on, Grandpa. Shoot a game with me.

GRANDPA

Oh, I don't know. I might've lost my touch.

Sound of footsteps going down the stairs.

ANNIE

Well, the lights are on. That's a good sign. Just a few more steps Grandpa.

GRANDPA

(*out of breath*) We'd come here all the time. We'd shoot a game after work to unwind, then we'd go next door to the Hoito for a home-cooked meal. Mashed potatoes and meatloaf. There were long tables and they'd set the food in the middle of the table in huge glass bowls. After a hard day's work in the bush, they put the food out. We ate it.

ANNIE

Didn't you and Grandma used to dip your toast in bacon grease?

GRANDPA

Yeah, well that was before they invented cholesterol. Now we have to watch everything. And we really have to watch your grandma especially.

ANNIE

Just a few more days and she'll be out of hospital, right?

GRANDPA

But who says for how long? She could end up back in the hospital too.

ANNIE

Oh, Grandpa, I think she'll be fine. She looked happy yesterday.

GRANDPA

She's always happy to see you.

ANNIE

So, where's all the cute guys you were talking about?

GRANDPA

I'm pretty cute for an eighty-four-year-old. At least your grand-ma thinks so. There's Harry. *(calling)* Hey Harry, me and my granddaughter are looking to shoot some pool. Can you set us up?

ANNIE

When my grandpa told Harry how my friends are musicians, he told us we could play a concert down there sometime if we wanted to. There's just something about finding an unexpected treasure in my old neighbourhood like this…. And my grandpa being the one to show me!

Uᵗʰ Ink
Orillia

**Community
Organizations**
Orillia and District
Arts Council

Playwright Facilitator
Shirley Barrie

Community Facilitator:
Lynn Fisher

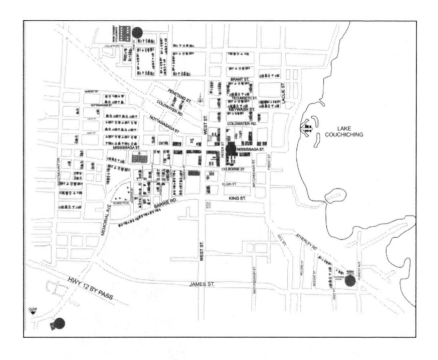

Each of the places marked with a dot on the map indicates a play's location.
Map illustrated by Xavier Fernandes

Buyout
Katie Nicholson

Site-Specific Location
Park Street Collegiate, 233 Park Street

ANNOUNCER
(*over the P.A. system*) …And tickets for the buyout for this afternoon's game will be sold at lunch today. Have a ttterifffic
Thursday.

MEL
Pft…. I hate when he says that.

MAGGIE
Hmm?

MEL
Tttterifffic Thursday, ick…. You really need to listen to the
announcements more. Are you going to the buyout?

MAGGIE
Buyout?

MEL
Yeah, during fourth. It's the senior boys' basketball team
playing.

MAGGIE
Fourth period? You gotta be serious. That's awesome!

MEL
Oooh. I see. Kaleb is captain and I think he likes y—

MAGGIE
No, I need to go to that game 'cause I have a math test and
that's in fourth. I didn't study.

MEL
Chill. Okay. At lunch we'll meet at the SAC office and we'll get
tickets. Okay?

MAGGIE

Sure. Just let me get through the rest of the day without freaking out.

Sounds of speaker buzzing.

(to herself) All right. Drama. It's close enough for me to make a run to the SAC office as soon as class is over. If I can just inch myself towards the door….

TEACHER

Maggie, you said you would stay behind and help clean up.

MAGGIE

Oh…. Okay. *(pause)* Jay! Can you clean up for me please? *(pause)* Pft. Loser. I gotta be quick.

Sounds of running.

All sold out?

ANNOUNCER

(over the P.A. system) Yeah, sorry.

MAGGIE

(to herself) Dang. I hope I can find Mel to get my ticket. Did she even get me one? What if I have to do the test? Ugh. I gotta find her quick. Just the usual crowd in the caf. I see some of her friends at the middle table. They tell me they haven't seen her. I race out to the hallway. It's all crowded with minor niners, but still no Mel. Maybe I'll take a peek into the library. Kinda like looking at the brief description on the back of a book. Hmmm. The librarian says that Mel came in after eleven. I'll zoom to Mel's locker at the far end of the hallway. Hmm. Well there's her friend from science class and her boyfriend making out. I'll just stand far a way's away to wait for the make-out session to be over with before I ask. Talk about awkward.

GIRL

(GIRL making out looks at MAGGIE and mutters.) Umm… try upstairs. *(GIRL plunges back into a romantic sequel with her boyfriend.)*

MAGGIE
> (*to herself*) The stairs up to the second floor are so cold. It's like climbing up a mountain. Hmm. I'll head down towards the languages hall where that group of girls is standing near the French class. The girls say that she just walked towards the gym.

> *Before leaving the group, MAGGIE steals a sip of one of the girls' chocolate milk to calm her nerves.*

> *MAGGIE takes a shortcut through the guidance services hall. The same hall shows all of the previous graduates.*

> They are all staring at me with those cheesy "Touch Photo" smiles.

> *MAGGIE enters the gym hall and hears calls. She peeks through the window in the door to see the senior boys rugby team practising. One of the boys gestures towards the back doors. MAGGIE races back to the front foyer to try and think where else to look when MEL appears through the front doors with a box of potato wedges from Zehrs.*

MEL
> Hey, Maggie. I got—

MAGGIE
> Do you have the tickets?

MEL
> Whagvd tikheyt?

MAGGIE
> Swallow before speaking a common language.

MEL
> What tickets?

MAGGIE
> The tickets that can get me out of a math doomsday!

MEL
> I gotta get to class early. Find me after at the library, I have to go.

Sound of speaker buzzing.

MAGGIE
(to herself in English class) English…. It's close enough to the library, but still…. Is English going to be like this for the whole period? It's like his words are purposefully slowing down time. *(pause)* So…. Bored…. Ugh. *(bell rings)* All right, I'm outta here. *(runs to the library)*

(irritated) Mel said that she would meet me at the library! Where is she?

MEL
Hey, Maggie.

MAGGIE
Do you have the tickets?

MEL
Yeah, here.

MAGGIE
Thanks.

MEL
You know, you do have to show the fourth period teacher the ticket.

MAGGIE
Crap.

MEL
Don't worry. I bet she'll let you go.

MAGGIE walks to math class to show her teacher the ticket.

MRS. KRAMER
Buyout? Hmm, Ms. Sampson? I think the team will have to miss their number one fan for a little test.

MAGGIE
What? Oh no, they need me, Mrs. Kramer. They're playing OD and they need all the support they can get.

MRS. KRAMER

Maggie, the game is—

MAGGIE

Is very important, Mrs. Kramer. I mean, it's the finals! So, I guess I'll start heading down—

MRS. KRAMER

I'm sorry, Maggie, but you need to do this test.

MAGGIE

Please! *(pause)* You're not going to let me go, are you?

MRS. KRAMER

Not a chance.

MAGGIE

Crap!

MRS. KRAMER

I think you want to leave because you didn't study for this test, right?

MAGGIE

Of course I studied!

MRS. KRAMER

You probably studied the latest conversations on Facebook rather than formulas to solving a math equation.

MAGGIE

Well…

MRS. KRAMER

I see. It's your choice. Leave and go to the game or…

MAGGIE

(excited) Oh, thank you!

MRS. KRAMER

Or you can lose fifteen percent of you final mark and feel really crummy.

MAGGIE

Will I get bonus points for being the only one here?

MRS. KRAMER

No, but I will remember this and I may accidentally skip some questions that were wrong.

MAGGIE

So, I did the test. The next day while the rest of the class fumed over the questions, I read a good novel, knowing I could have been in the same boat.

Irresistible Opposites
Storme Garwood

Site-Specific Location
Mariposa Market

> *This play takes place at Mariposa Market in Orillia. It's quiet, with the occasional chatter of families and couples. This scene starts with NICOLE and STEPHANIE talking. STEPHANIE has just broken it off with yet another man.*

NICOLE
Back again, Stephanie? It seems to me like any time you break it off with a guy, you come in here and order a large hot chocolate with extra whipped cream.

STEPHANIE
Oh, Nicole, you're right. The extra whipped cream seems to help. But it's not only that, it's the place. I mean, look around… couples, families, everyone seems so happy. Why can't I have that?

NICOLE
(half-heartedly) Oh, Tristan wasn't all that bad.

STEPHANIE
(laughing to herself) For some reason a thirty-year-old guy still living with his mother doesn't quite appeal to me. Can you imagine he was happy with that? I knew after he didn't want to get a place together it was time to break it off. I was looking for a husband, Nicole, not a child. Uh, what was I thinking? I don't know, it just seems like love is non-existent for me. Well, thanks for the hot chocolate.

NICOLE
That's what I'm here for. Oh, hi, Frank. What can I get for…

FRANK
Who is she?

NICOLE

(confused) I'm sorry?

FRANK

That woman you were just talking to. Who is she? What's her name?

NICOLE

Oh, she's a friend. (shrugging her shoulders) Why?

FRANK

Do you believe in love at first sight?

NICOLE

For most people, yes I do, but for you, Frank, (pause and then chuckles) I never knew you were capable of love.

FRANK

(ignoring NICOLE) Oh, I think this might be the one.

NICOLE

(sarcastically) Okay, Romeo. Look, I wouldn't even try, she's going through another breakup of hers, and let's just say you're not her type.

FRANK

Of course I'm her type. I'm everyone's type. Well, here it goes. (approaches STEPHANIE) Hi, is this seat taken?

STEPHANIE

Excuse me? Oh (laughs) I see. I'm not looking for a relationship right now, thanks.

FRANK

Good thing I just want to talk then.

STEPHANIE

Did Nicole put you up to this?

FRANK

Not at all. She actually told me I'd be wasting my time.

STEPHANIE

And, no offence, she's right.

FRANK
Hmm. Well, why don't we meet back here *(pause)* let's see, around noon on Saturday, nothing fancy and no commitment.

STEPHANIE
That's awfully kind of you, but let's be honest here, I don't know you.

FRANK
Well, my name is Frank, I'm thirty-three years old and I own my own company. I'm straight, single, like going to movies, hate caviar and love swimming at the beach. I guess you should also know that I own my own home in Horseshoe Valley. Is there anything else?

STEPHANIE
(hesitantly) I.... Uh.... I guess that pretty much covers it.

FRANK
Great, then I'll see you Saturday. Bye.

STEPHANIE
(in shock) Bye.

STEPHANIE
Nicole, did I just agree to have lunch with that guy?

NICOLE
I can't believe it, but you did. What's the harm? You come in here all the time anyway. I'm a little surprised that you said yes.

STEPHANIE
Yeah, you're right, I mean.... I love caviar and I can't even swim.

NICOLE
Hey, opposites attract, right?

Tim Hortons
Jake Thompson

Site-Specific Location

Tim Hortons, 265 Atherley Road

ACTOR ONE

(dry, thickened vocal chords) Ahhh food. I, I need food. *(with obvious pain)* I must get to Orillia, home of the Tim Hortons...

ACTOR TWO

(over-optimistic voice) Well my friend, you're in luck. You're already in Orillia. Just turn around this here corner and whoaoaahaahooo, Tim Hortons.

ACTOR ONE

Wow, that's weird. I've heard of things like this happening in Orillia before. Well, I'm going to order something. Hello, Tim Hortons. Yes, thank you. One Timbit. Yep, glazed with sugar. All right, I... *(with mounting horror)* Oh my God. There's no sugar on this thing.

ACTOR TWO

(shocked tone) Oh my God, really?

ACTOR ONE

(sarcastically) Of course not. How could such an amazing place hold such a flaw. *(sighs)*

ACTOR TWO

Ah, how true you are, my friend. What a place. It holds such memories for me... *(fades off)*

ACTOR ONE

Oh no, you're not going to launch into one of those daydream recollections that sound like advertisements for Tim Hortons, are you?

ACTOR TWO

It all started long ago when I was very young...

ACTOR ONE
Oh no.

ACTOR TWO
I was sitting in one of my favourite places, Tim Hortons. One day while I was idly sucking on an Iced Cap, a young man came through the door and ordered a small coffee and a dough-nut.

ACTOR ONE
Hmmm. He's got good taste.

ACTOR TWO
Ssshh…. He sat down at a table close to mine and contentedly started eating his purchase when a woman burst through the door. Hesitantly following her was a young girl covered in freckles, hiding behind her mother's back. The woman proceeded to a counter upon which a plastic plant…

ACTOR ONE
Ahhh, those plastic plants. They have it in for us all. I just really don't get them. Why not just buy real plants?

ACTOR TWO
Ahheemm. *(annoyed at ACTOR ONE for continuously interrupting)* Where was I? Ahh yes…. And ordered a small package of Timbits for her child and a coffee for herself and sat down at the only table left, which happened to be the table the man was sitting at.

ACTOR ONE
Only one table? Hmmm, must've been one of those days.

ACTOR TWO
"Do you mind if we join you?" The woman asked. The man shook his head no and the woman and her daughter sat down and the woman started to talk. They found that they were both from the same town. At the mention of this town's name the man stared off into space and a dreamy look appeared in his eyes. "Why are you looking off like that?" the young woman said. The man replied, "I met the love of my life there, but when we were young she had to move to Brookvale." Now the

woman stiffened. "Wh… what was her name?" she asked. "Rebecca." the man replied with love in his eyes. The woman turned away as her eyes filled with tears then turned back. "I… I am Rebecca." The man took the words in as if trying to process them. "But… but you have a child," he said. "Yes," she said. "I'm married." The man slumped back into his chair. The woman rose, and after telling him she had to go, walked sadly out into the rain with her daughter trailing behind her. Her tears mixed with the falling rain and the man mournfully watched her walk away. I went up to the man shortly after and said, "Mister, I heard everything, I… I'm so sorry." He didn't say anything, so I turned and left. Just as I was going out the door he called out, "Kid…" I turned around. "Thanks," he said. I nodded and walked away.

ACTOR ONE
Wow, that's intense. Thanks for telling me that.

ACTOR TWO
No problem, thank Tim Hortons for its strange ability to bring people together. *(pause)* So, what brings you here?

ACTOR ONE
To Orillia? Well, I'll tell you if you buy me an Iced Cap.

ACTOR TWO
Oh, well, okay.

ACTOR ONE
Wow, really? Gee thanks. Oh my God. My Iced Cap isn't frozen.

Bro and I
Harry Cleaveley

Site-Specific Location

700 Memorial Avenue

After a long night of drinking.

DAVID

Do you mind if I sit and wait here with you?

MARY

No, go ahead. *(sipping her coffee)* So, what are you here for?

DAVID

Well, ever since my brother died, alcohol has become my new stress reliever. I know it's not good, but now I have no one to discuss my problems with. My brother was the only one I trusted my secrets with. We used to do everything together. Like play ball down at Tudhope Park, go downtown for pizza.

My older brother was quite the guy. I can still remember the day when we were standing outside of the Orillia Opera House. My brother saw this girl sitting on a bench near the public library. I could tell by his face that he had a crush on her. You could see the sweat dripping from his forehead. I knew they were meant for each other. Every few seconds you would see their eyes connect. Then they would look away with mini smiles on their faces. That was the first time I ever saw my brother act mature around a lady. Let me tell you, it was nice to see my brother not acting like the big shot for once.

That day meant a lot to me, just because my brother and I bonded so well. But now he's gone, and it's all because I didn't leave the car keys on the table. *(pause)*

I should have been the one that died in the accident. After all, I was the one drinking and driving like a nutcase. Why didn't I just listen to my friends and just stay the night at their place. Then I wouldn't be in this awful mess. *(starts to cry)* My brother didn't even have any say. He was so smashed and out of it. He didn't even know what was going on.

Well, I guess I deserve to get locked up for this. After all, life isn't going to be the same without bro here. I can just picture what the judge is going to say to me when I get inside. Well, there's my lawyer, Ted, waving me into the courtroom. I guess I better go and face up to what I've done.

Oh, and thanks for listening to me.

MARY
Mary. (*gesturing towards herself*)

DAVID
It meant a lot.

MARY
No problem, and good luck.

DAVID gives MARY a little grin and walks away.

Uth Ink Etobicoke

Community Organizations
Lakeshore Arts

Playwright Facilitator
Kathleen McDonnell

Community Facilitator
Melissa McGrath

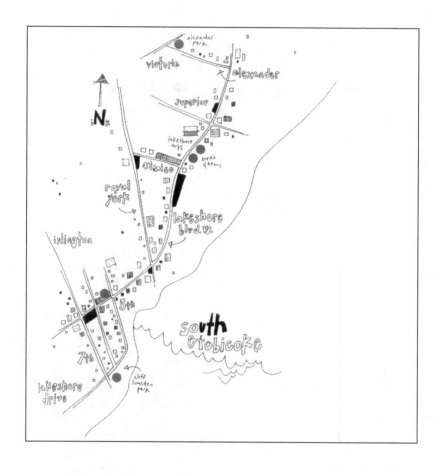

Each of the places marked with a dot on the map indicates a play's location.
Map illustrated by Melissa McGrath

Toxic
Dawson Bonneville

Site-Specific Location
Cliff Lumsden Park

DAWSON

If you are hearing this you are standing in Cliff Lumsden Park. In 1905 a filtration plant was made here in this park. One day, a man who worked at the station named Walter Hemmingway was carrying two vials filled with nuclear testing liquid. Some people say he simply slipped into the lake and dropped them in accidentally. Other people believe that he was pushed or he even poured them in purposely. But either way he fell into the lake holding the vials, no one really knows how.

There was one witness to the accident and that was a man by the name of Victor Treble. Victor spoke to the newspaper saying that he saw one of the biggest phenomena of the twentieth century. "It was like flash fire," said Victor. He stated that the vials Walter was carrying were DNA testing fluids for research related to the defections of animals in southern Cuba. Once the fluids fell into the lake they created a flash of fire across the lake, but only for a second or two. Walter fell into the lake after the fluids had already had their effect. Victor said that he ran to help him, but then fled when Walter came out of the lake with two extra arms.

Just as anyone would imagine, as soon as this hit newspapers people from all over the earth would come to this lake seeking "super powers." Science fiction movies were big at the time and people wanted to be "super." People with incurable sicknesses would take a dive to try and rid themselves of diseases. These parts you're standing in right now were constantly packed with hundreds of people. A year or so after Walter's first accident he came down with a terrible sickness. Newspapers were head-lined "EVACUATE ETOBICOKE" for fear of nuclear radiation. Any person who ever jumped into this lake became deathly ill and hospitals were beginning to overpack with very sick patients. Years passed by and nuclear specialists trying to remove the toxins quarantined this lake. People started to protest in front of the lake, telling the scientists that this lake was a gift and these mutations are just a way of life. "God brought us these miracles!" This enraged the government of Canada and they felt they needed to step in. People strangely stopped talking about the lake's powers and it never once appeared in newspapers. The government quietly destroyed all evidence and hushed victims. If you can see the fountain in the park now, it will tell you that was the main filtration unit at the past station. If you walk closer towards the lake you will see the remains of the factory. No one ever spoke of this after 1930 and the world remains completely quiet about this entire event.

You might be wondering how I found out about all this. One day while walking through the park, I found a box sitting on a bench with a note on top of it. This note told about the box's contents and briefly described the situation. The box contained many newspapers and file documents about the lake and Walter Hemmingway. This note was signed Timothy Hemmingway, Walter's grandson.

The Dog in My Head
Laina Timberg

<u>Site-Specific Location</u>
Birds and Beans, 2413 Lakeshore Boulevard West

Café sounds: coffee slurps, soft chatter. Door opens and a dog barks.

GIRL
(*thinking to herself*) The poor dog, outside in the cold. She looks so sad. I wish I could bring her in here and get her all warm.

DOG
If you really want to help me, bring me inside. I hate the cold. The summer is a lot more fun. If you bring me in, I could get something nice and warm to drink—perhaps a chai tea?

GIRL
Wait, I'm talking to a dog in my head? I must be hearing things.

DOG
No, you are not hearing things. I am a dog and I am talking to you in your head. I want to talk to you, so I am. End of story. Now, would you mind untying me so I can come into that warm café that you are enjoying?

GIRL
You're not my dog. I can't untie you. I'd get in a lot of trouble!

DOG
So? Does it really matter that I am not your dog?

GIRL
Yeah, it does. People will think I'm stealing you.

DOG
Not if I am injured. You would be helping me if I'm injured. Oh, look, I am falling over. I will hit the ground very soon. (*thunk sound*) Oh, there, I hit the ground.

MAN

Is that my dog, playing dead again? She'll do anything for attention when I'm not with her.

GIRL

Is that your owner? He doesn't hear you?

DOG

What happened? I feel very faint. Oh, look! My eyes are closing. I can hardly see.

GIRL

Am I the only one who can hear you? Oh my gosh, that's so weird.

DOG

Woof! Oh, someone help me, I am injured. You must bring me inside—someplace warm, like this café right here!

GIRL

I can't bring you in. Dogs aren't allowed in cafés.

DOG

No, I will be allowed. The owners really like birds, so they must like dogs. Everyone likes dogs. Dogs and birds go so well together. They are a matching pair, so the owners have to like dogs if they like birds.

GIRL

Listen, I'm really sorry, but I can't help you. Look, your owner's finished his coffee. He'll be out in a minute and before you know it, you'll be back at your house, all nice and warm.

DOG

Yes, after the long walk back home through the bitter cold.

GIRL

Walking is good for you.

DOG

I will get ice in my pads. I will go lame, and you will be responsible.

Sound of footsteps. A bell chimes. A door opens with a rush of air.

MAN

Oh, Maya, stop playing dead! Come on, we're going home.

DOG

Woof woof! Yes, home! I can hardly wait. Come on, time is ticking. I want to get to the warmth and my food and…

GIRL

Wait, what about me? You're just going to leave me here? After you tried to get me to come outside and bring you into the café?

DOG

Ah, yes. What else would I do? Take you home with me? You are already in a nice warm place. Now I must get to mine. Goodbye. Oh, and come back next Saturday and we can do this again. Twelve noon. Don't be late!

MAN

Maya, come on. Don't you want to get home?

The dog barks.

Time Concealed is Finally Unsealed
Veronica Brown

<u>   Site-Specific Location</u>
Alexander Park

YOUNG GIRL

May 3rd, 2102. Dear Diary: The most incredible thing happened today. I found a time capsule! I was playing with my friends and we noticed a box with an old metal plaque on it sticking out from underneath a giant rock. We could read the words on the plaque—it said: "Alexander Park Rejuvenation Project 2002." 2002—that was a hundred years ago! Back then there must have been a park right here. Of course, now, like every-where else in Toronto, this is a condominium complex. Inside the box there was a photo of David Hornell Junior School, the school that used to be nearby. It seemed so small, it could have only gone to grade five or six. Today our schools go to grade twelve, at least.

The contents of the time capsule were quite odd. There was some kind of toy called a Beyblade. The instructions said you had to pull on something to make it spin. I found this kind of strange because today our toys take care of themselves: no pushing, pulling, winding or wheeling. There were also a few colourful, very long tubes that my grandmother told me were called skipping ropes. I think kids played with them at school and in the park, kind of jumping over them. But skipping ropes haven't been made or used for at least fifty years now.

I was fascinated by the scrapbook in the time capsule. It had all the class photos from 2002 glued in, and kids had written in it with an old-fashioned pen. The kids dressed so differently than we do now. They wore these blue pants on their legs—jeans, I think they were called—and many kids liked to wear bright colours. Now, we can only wear outfits of silver-toned material to protect us from the sun's damaging rays. I noticed that many children in the photos had braces. My grandparents had them too. Today, in the year 2102, people have no need for braces because after many generations we have become genetically adapted to have perfectly aligned teeth.

We also found an old newspaper with a photo showing large teams of people in bright T-shirts building the park. They appear to be smiling—like building it was fun or something. It was all done in one day, but they had spent the whole year before that raising money. Another photo showed a small group of children standing in front of a green sign. The caption reads "A revolutionary project called Murmur comes to Mimico." Hmmm, sounds intriguing.

Looking at the things in the time capsule made me wish that I could visit the year 2002. It looks like such a nice time. Now Toronto is so crowded, and the population has almost doubled. It's a good thing there are at least a few parks left under domes, otherwise kids wouldn't even know what it is was like to just have fun, to run and be carefree, to hang out with your friends and your family and enjoy your community. It was so interesting to see and hear what our ancestors did for fun. Well, that's all for now, Diary. Till tomorrow…

       Love,

Zindra Orion Stardust

A Streetcar Named Long Branch
Bianca Chelu-Penalagan

Site-Specific Location
Birds and Beans, 2413 Lakeshore Boulevard West

> *A streetcar stops. Footsteps are heard getting off the streetcar and then continue as two children, one about nine or ten (LEANNE), the other about fourteen or fifteen (GEMMA) walk along the sidewalk.*

LEANNE
Mommy said you have to be nice to me, Gemma. You're not supposed to go and hang out with your friends! We're just supposed to go to the 7-Eleven and then come back home.

GEMMA
Yeah, whatever, Leanne.

LEANNE
I'll tell Mommy on you if you don't listen!

GEMMA
Oh, I'm so scared. Like I actually care, Leanne.

LEANNE
(mumbling) I will. *(louder)* Where are we going right now, anyway? For real I mean?

GEMMA
We're going to Birds and Beans. Seriously, Leanne, we go there all the time, where else would we be going?

LEANNE
Well, 7-Eleven, since that's what you told Mommy! I don't want to go to Birds and Beans anyways. All you do is buy drinks with your friends and ignore me the whole time and then lie to Mommy when we get home!

GEMMA
So what? You're just jealous 'cause I have friends and you don't.

LEANNE
That's not true! I'm not jealous of you! And I do have friends!

GEMMA
(laughing) Oh yeah? Like who?

LEANNE
Jennifer, Madeline, Sarah, Libby, Diana, John, Markus…

GEMMA
(cutting LEANNE off) Wow, Leanne, you're so cool! I mean, why can't I be friends with the biggest loser in school? *(laughs)* Isn't Libby like, the one with the weird haircut? You know, how her hair is always gelled up into those weird spiky ponytail things, and she wears those disgusting salmon-coloured pants!

LEANNE
Shut up, Gemma! My friends aren't losers.

GEMMA
I mean, her hair's almost as bad as yours. Did she, like, help you dye it that ugly red colour and put those ultra cool pigtails in?

LEANNE
There's nothing wrong with my hair! You're the loser, Gemma! At least my friends and I are original!

GEMMA
Ouch, Leanne, that really hurts. I'm sorry we're not original or cool enough for you and your friends.

LEANNE
You know what, Gemma? Just leave me alone! I'm not going with you to Birds and Beans! I'm going to…. I'm going for a walk!

GEMMA
Fine, be stupid! I don't care what you do! Just go away. I don't like you anyway. I'd much rather hang out with my friends!

LEANNE
Fine! *(LEANNE storms off.)*

GEMMA

Hey, where are you going? We're, like, right here! I'll buy you
something, I promise! Get back here, Leanne! Right now! I'm
going to get in so much trouble!

LEANNE

I don't care how much trouble you get in! I told you I'm going
for a walk!

GEMMA

(to herself) Oh, whatever…

*Footsteps are heard running away. The sound of a door being opened
is heard. Quiet talking is also heard. Two new characters, MARIA and
TANYA, are introduced.*

MARIA

Gemma!

TANYA

Oh, wow, hey, Gemma! What's up?

GEMMA

Oh, hey, Maria, hey, Tanya!

TANYA

I saw Leanne run away. Something wrong?

GEMMA

Ugh. Nothing. Leanne was just being dumb, as usual.

MARIA

Ha. Leanne is an angel compared to my brother. You should
have seen what he did this morning! My mom, Kelly and I were
all sitting at the table eating breakfast. My dad didn't have to
work, so he decided to make us pancakes, which were sooo
good by the way. But anyway, Michael bangs down the stairs,
rushes into the kitchen and slams right into the table!

TANYA

Aw, that sucks!

GEMMA

What happened then?

MARIA

Well, that made the milk go flying, and you know where it landed? Right on...

Screeching of a car trying to get its breaks on quickly, followed by a loud scream.

GEMMA

Oh my gosh! What was that?

TANYA

I think there was an accident! Let's go see!

Background commotion. People are heard exclaiming "What happened?" "I hope no one's hurt."

Sound of the café door opening and footsteps going out. Sound of an ambulance.

GEMMA

Oh, no! Someone's been hit!

TANYA

I hope they're okay!

MARIA

Can you see who it is?

TANYA

Nope. It must be a girl, though.... I mean, what boy wears pigtails in his hair? *(laughing)* Especially ones so high up?

GEMMA

(in a panicky voice) Wait. What did you say?

MARIA

Oh, nothing. Just that whoever that is has no sense of hair styling whatsoever. And, I'm sorry, but who is stupid enough to step in front of a car? It's called a cross*walk*!

TANYA

Ha, I know, right, Gemma?

GEMMA

(almost speechless) I... I...

MARIA

Gemma?

Back Where I Belong
Pamela Vazquez Moreno

<u>Site-Specific Location</u>
Lakeshore Boulevard West at Fifth Street

MELISSA

It all started here, in this same place where my grandmother was first kidnapped by aliens, the same spot where I was kidnapped by the aliens too. When I was a girl, every day after school I'd go running to my grandparents' house to hear about how the aliens came from space and took her to their planet. But after years of hearing the same story over and over, I started to lose interest. Her stories were so mythological they seemed like Santa Claus stories, and I no longer had a little kid's innocence. My grandfather said that she was crazy and that she made up silly stories after her heart failure. But my grandmother insisted that she really meant them. Her face had such a look of amazement and her words sounded so truthful that I believed her even though at the end she'd always say "It's only a story."

When I turned fifteen, my grandmother died. Her last words to me were, "If you believe me, go to Lakeshore and Fifth Street, I have a surprise for you." She never said why, when, with whom, or anything at all. I often passed this street, and I always remembered my grandmother's words. But I thought it would look weird to go and just stand there, waiting for something to happen. So, I resisted the impulse to go and look. I just knew I would never find anything. Until one day I heard a phrase in a song that changed my mind.

ALIZ

If you never try, you never know.

MELISSA

That's when I decided to come here and see if I could find something. I found a rock. Strangely enough, it caught my eye.

ALIZ

And then you threw it and everything started.

MELISSA

Yes, that's when everything started. The sky was clear, a freezing wind chilled my back and the sound of the lake came into my ears. Night became day in a minute. A red light illuminated the sky and everything around me. I thought I must be dreaming, but everything was true. The wind grew stronger and the trees started to bend. All of a sudden I felt small electrical charges from head to toe. I felt light and I started to float. I felt free. I saw everything floating too—stones, benches, cats, dogs, anything but humans. I was the only one floating. As I looked at the horizon, the city seemed kind of lonely. The red light reflected in every window of the CN Tower and every wave on the lake, making a reflection of light. It was like the sun turned red. In the sky I could see the clouds, but it was like we didn't have the ozone. I could see the universe, the stars, the planets, everything! It was just beautiful and peaceful. Suddenly there was a very sharp sound, breaking every glass and striking me deaf. Then waves of electricity ran through my body, making me bend over in pain. I was floating alone, wondering "Why me?" The electric shocks came again, though I didn't feel them so strongly anymore. It felt like positive energy entered my body. Although I felt at peace, I hoped it would end soon. I remember every sound and movement seemed so slow, and my vision started to blur. I felt so weak I just closed my eyes and went unconscious.

I fainted. I opened my eyes and I still couldn't see anything. I started to freak. Then I heard your voice, calming me down.

ALIZ

(*makes a little laugh*) You know we are the ones who made you.

MELISSA

Yes, I know, but I want to go back to my world.

ALIZ

You are in your world, in another dimension. Every voice you hear is a person you know.

MELISSA

Then who are you?

ALIZ

I can't tell you. If I tell you, everything could end.

MELISSA

But I want it to end.

ALIZ

Oh! You are just like your mother! You have to understand…

MELISSA

What? I want to go back to where I belong! I want to be with the people I love and who love me back!

ALIZ

You are with the people you love. Just feel our presence and calm down, you are starting to be annoying.

MELISSA

How can I calm myself knowing my world is in danger, all because of me? And I don't know where the hell I am! And I'm blind!

ALIZ

No, Melissa, you didn't cause any danger. You went into the future. You only felt pain when you died, but don't worry, you are with the ones you really love and who love you back. You are safe. Everything that you saw you imagined. We used your imagination to transport you.

MELISSA

But… where is my future? Or where is my past? So, nothing happened?

ALIZ

You'll remember little by little. You lived a full life. We just make you feel young so you have energy to pass through this. Just trust us. We know who you are. In a couple of months you'll have your vision back. We think it is dangerous if you see everything at once. I still can't believe that you haven't mentioned your grandmother, not even her stories.... I feel offended.

MELISSA

Grandmother?

ALIZ

Yes, dear?

MELISSA

Will it end? *(appearing a little worried)*

ALIZ

No, I was just making things interesting.

MELISSA

So.... If I am dead, where is God? Am I in heaven?

ALIZ

(laughing) No, dear. Such a thing doesn't happen here. If you behave nicely to the people you are surrounded with, you'll meet them in your afterlife, but if you treat everyone hurtfully, if you are selfish or mean, you'll meet their essence in your death. Most of the time you meet with the person you missed and loved the most.

MELISSA

Essence?

ALIZ

Yes, Mel, you weren't gonna come with that old, flubby, wrinkled, decomposed body, were you?

MELISSA

I feel my body.

ALIZ

Oh yeah. I almost forgot. You have another body, hope you like it.

MELISSA

But.... If I got married... why not my husband or children?

ALIZ

Well, because in our conscience and deep memories we sometimes love the people of our childhood more. It's more pure and
innocent.... I mean, you are lucky, some people meet with their
lovers.... You never know...

MELISSA

Where is my family?

ALIZ

In time you'll meet them. You have to be ready.

MELISSA

How long will this last?

ALIZ

We don't have the same time here.

MELISSA

Can I touch you?

ALIZ

Not now, you still have to be ready.

MELISSA

Then I fainted again. I woke up in the same old bed, in the
same old world, with this same old body.

GRANDSON

Grandma, do you really believe?

MELISSA

Of course, it happened to me.

GRANDSON

But it's only a story.

MELISSA

Yes, it's only a story.

Uth Ink
Sudbury

**Community
Organizations**
Myths and Mirrors
Community Arts

Playwright Facilitator
Marjorie Chan

Community Facilitator
Tina Roy

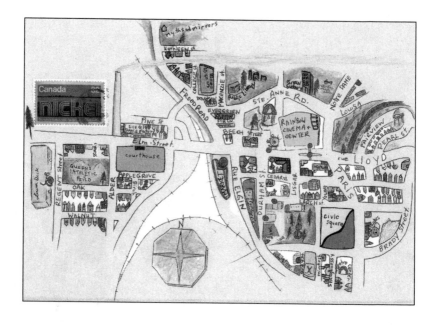

Each of the places marked with a dot on the map indicates a play's location.
Map illustrated by Tanya Ball

The Orthodontist, the Coffee Shop and the Apartment
Meagan Mullally

<u>Site-Specific Location</u>

81 Larch Street

MEAGAN at age twelve at the orthodontist.

DENTIST

What colour elastics do you want this time?

MEAGAN

(to herself) I have the smallest teeth on earth and now they are entirely covered in giant metal brackets.

…uhm… blue, I guess.

(to herself) My teeth weren't that crooked to begin with. I look like an idiot.

DENTIST

All right, let's see how they're doing.

MEAGAN

(to herself) They were only supposed to be on for a few months, but every time I come back here the orthodontist tells me it will be another few until finally it's been what feels like years. Good enough yet?

The braces come off.

DENTIST

Worth it, huh? Look at how straight they are.

MEAGAN

(to herself) I can laugh without putting my hands over my mouth.

Yeah, I guess they are.

(to herself) I can smile broadly and not feel embarrassed by the
bits of metal which once protruded from my face.

DENTIST

See you for a checkup in six months.

MEAGAN

Upon revisiting the orthodontist's office, I'm informed that,
much to my dismay, I would need braces again.

You've got to be kidding!

I never went back.

MEAGAN at age fifteen in the coffee shop.

(to herself) The Dark Room is... well, exactly what it sounds like.

Hey!

(to herself) The darkly painted and dimly lit internet café was
truly a haven for some.

FRIEND

Hey, want to share a bagel?

MEAGAN

(to herself) I found comfort in the haze of cigarette smoke and
cups of vanilla tea.

Sure. What are you reading?

(to herself) We talked about all kinds of things while sipping and
smoking.

FRIEND

I'm learning to read palms.

MEAGAN

(to herself) Punk music, art, politics, vegetarianism, feminism,
tarot readings.

Whoa, do mine.

(to herself) Years later the Dark Room shuts down and is
replaced by some new hangout. It isn't the same.

FRIEND

Looks like you will live a long life…. Have lots of kids…. But you'll be alone.

MEAGAN

(to herself) I never once step foot into the café's successor.

Wicked, I can hardly wait!

(to herself) I never went back.

MEAGAN at age twenty-one in an apartment that is down the hall from the orthodontist's office, which is now vacant and upstairs from the Dark Room, which is now a pharmaceutical distributor.

(to herself) Ironically enough, all these years later I move into an apartment in this building.

This building never smells the same. You know how buildings always have a smell. This place doesn't.

FRIEND

Are all the other rooms in here dental offices?

MEAGAN

(to herself) For a plethora of reasons, which I won't revisit here, I lived there for a little less than a week.

Pretty much. Dentist, dentist, urologist, dentist…

(to herself) My friends live there now.

FRIEND

Looks fun in here!

MEAGAN

(to herself) I visit frequently.

Yeah. We all had a hand in decorating it.

(to herself) I crash on the couch.

FRIEND

And you guys all get together for dinner?

MEAGAN

(to herself) I go to dinner parties on Sundays.

Every Sunday!

(to herself) I never left.

The Four Chambers of the Heart of Sudbury
Matt Moskal

<u>Site-Specific Location</u>
At the corner of Durham Street and Elm Street

MATT

Hi! Welcome to the intersection of Durham and Elm. I never could actually identify the heart of Sudbury until the internet came into the picture. I discovered this location from a completely different angle than I was used to when I looked it up a while back. I looked it up on Google, under images. And there was a completely different perspective, a completely different view than I was used to getting off the bus. There's a bus station right down Elm there and I would take a pathway up past Grand and Toy and up to Casa Mexicana. I never considered doing it the other way, which seems kind of odd and slightly ignorant. This just inspired me to explore Sudbury from that point on. Seeing this image and seeing how glorious this street looked from another point of view, I went ahead. Every adventure, I'd start from that point and discover a different aspect of the city. I've been looking for the perfect cup of coffee in the city, and actually, if you take one of these four different roads from here, you will find it. I'm not going to tell you where it is because that's your personal mission upon hearing this story— is to find this coffee. To find this glorious, satisfying, thick, well-brewed beverage to wake yourself up in the morning, and you will thank me for it in the back of your mind, hopefully.

You have a lot of history in this corner here. You have a local business if you look to the… well I'm not sure which way you're looking. If you look to your side and you see a nice white delightful sign, you have one of the longest running businesses in all of Sudbury, where local gossip flourishes and music is played, and where I found some of my favourite albums I'd ever heard in my life. Ignoring this business would be a mistake at this point in time. Definitely a fantastic venture to even just go in and throw two dollars down on a record and bring it home to find your old record player. Let the night take you wherever. I'm not saying do something spontaneous. We've all got work in the morning. But there's a lot of interesting times that can be had or inspired simply by throwing two dollars down on a counter and seeing where that takes you.

Spontaneous Dance Party
Tina Roy

Site-Specific Location
Durham Street, beside the YMCA

TINA

(speaking loudly) It's a bit loud in here. Come out into the hallway with me for a second.

Door closes and muffles out the party.

You should have been here…. Man oh man, you really should have been here! You can ask Meagan and Jen about it. It was so amazing! The three of us arrived here at my apartment one night, and within only a few minutes a bunch of people appeared at my door with armfuls of wine and good drink. Everyone was in a spectacular mood that night, the lighting in my place was just right and two different circles of friends of mine came together as one around my kitchen table as I searched for the perfect record to play. Bob Marley? No. UB40? No, not them either. Hmmm. Come to think of it, I can't remember which one I put on, but I remember that everyone liked it. After I had stopped fiddling with the bass and treble, and stopped worrying about what I would play next, I looked up and around the room to find everyone dancing! Every single person there was grooving to the music, smiling ear to ear and having a blast. One of the first parties I ever hosted here in Sudbury was already a hit, and all I had to do was lower the needle of the record player and turn up the volume.

Door opens, a person steps out.

PERSON

Hey! What are you doing out here in the hall. There's a great party happening in there!

TINA

I was just telling Patty about the last party I had here.

PERSON

Is that the one where we actually got to see Judy dancing? Man, that was great. You really should have been there!

Arts Corner
Bodicca Mitchell

Site-Specific Location

19 Grey Street

BODICCA

So, you've arrived at 19 Grey and you're curious. Well, are you ready for a stroll? Good. If you walk up this street to about the middle, keep looking at the ground you'll discover a manhole cover. Do you see it? If you walk over a little closer, you will see a date... 1915.

So, this building has been around quite a long time. It used to be a karate studio. Then it was a film production studio. After that it became an artist residence. And now it's T.A.G & Film.

I guess you could say that this place has been a little bit of an addition to the cultural downtown of Sudbury. Artists coming and going and always creating something.

Whether it be art or just a good time. My partner and I opened T.A.G in autumn of 2007. If you look at the building you may still see our sign. If so, we're still open and you should definitely stop by and say hello.

We've got a ton more stories to tell you in person. So, T.A.G. We wanted it to be a house of art with art films and a giant gallery space to display the local colour of Sudbury's art talent. Visual, musical or whatever.

We've had all sorts of shows here. Nights of music, nights of poetry and especially nights of art.

For our second show we organized a communal show of fifteen local artists called Made In Sudbury. It was certainly quite the scene. I think over the entire night we had about a hundred and twenty people stop by. There was singing and laughing. Chit and chat and more chit chat...

That night the streets were abuzz with the opening. Artists of all sorts and fabulous patrons who just happened to be in the area stopped by for some wine and cheese and great art.

People were stopping by from dinner at the Buddha, just up the street on Elgin.

People were coming in from the Townehouse, which you'll notice is just up the street on your right. On the corner of Elgin and Grey. A wild scene, definitely worth reminiscing about.

So, that show was quite the success.

One other time, Elton John came to town to do a show at the Sudbury Arena. It was one of the grossest rainy nights. Wet and cold. But a bunch of our friends and us stood right outside this door and saw Mr. Elton come out of the arena. If you look right across the street there are the big doors of the Sudbury Arena. Those are the doors. Elton John, red carpet, big black SUV and all! Crazy, huh!

Sudbury Arts Corner, for sure.

Snowed In
Codie Fortin Lalonde

Site-Specific Location
Townehouse Tavern, 206 Elgin Street

Sounds of walking and cars passing.

PERSON
Oh, hey! Where are you heading?

CODIE
Hey! I'm on my way to the bus depot.

PERSON
Oh, me too.

CODIE
How come you didn't come to the show?

PERSON
Well, it was a Sunday night and the weather was really bad.

CODIE
You must have known there was going to be a snow day for Monday. It snowed like two feet!

PERSON
Yeah, was it good though?

CODIE
Yes! It was amazing. You know how Dear Jane was supposed to play last? Well, they were really late because of the snowstorm, but everyone stayed anyway. Then when they got there, they told us about how they almost died three times trying to get from Toronto to Sudbury. They almost hit a transport!

PERSON
So they played a good show?

CODIE
Yeah, it was so good. The whole thing. There was so much

energy in the room. Everyone was super excited about it. And you know how it's so tiny, so the whole place was just vibrating. I lifted my foot about an inch off the floor and I could feel the vibrations hitting my foot. Then everyone saw me doing it and did it too. *(laughs)*

PERSON

Wow, I missed out, didn't I?

CODIE

Totally.

PERSON

Man, that sucks! I should have gone!

CODIE

(laughs) Too late now, eh?

PERSON

Well, how did everyone get home?

CODIE

I don't really know. My bus was the last bus they sent out and we almost slid into the mall trying to get out of the station! It was so crazy. But it was worth it. I had a blast.

PERSON

Whoa.

Fight for Your Life
Alice Norquay

Site-Specific Location

Elm Street, the crosswalk between the mall and the bus depot

ALICE

Okay. So, here we are, at the tightrope walk of crosswalks in Sudbury. Notice the superb placement between the mall and the bus depot. Super heavy pedestrian traffic all the time. And not just any pedestrians. For some odd reason this is the one place where all the rudest, least conscientious pedestrians congregate. It frustrates drivers to no end when someone jumps out in front of their vehicle for no apparent reason. *(yelling driver in background)* I should know, because oftentimes I am one of said frustrated drivers.

I don't understand it. Is there some rumour that cars are really a hallucination, and roads are really for everyone to wander all over? Do people think that my crummy little car can stop faster than their obviously quick feet? Do they think that they'll come out on top in a physical confrontation between the two? Or maybe it's an odd death wish. Because really, basic sense 101: Look before you cross the street!

And so, let us make the trek together...

Improvise crossing the street.

Honky Tonk Friday
Matt Ralph

Site-Specific Location

Lower Deck bar, 19 Regent Street

MATT

One of my most memorable adventures with my friends in Sudbury has taken place right here at the Lower Deck. It all began rather strangely, actually.

Four or five of us got fish-hooked into attending a very intimate cleansing circle for a mutual friend. Now, I'm not sure if every cleansing circle feels like twenty funerals going on all at once in the smallest, stuffiest room known to mankind, but this one sure did. After what seemed like hours of awkwardness, the night seemed to be drawing to a close when suddenly a random cowboy burst into the room with his mandolin and proceeded to serenade us all. He informed us that he would be playing a show here at the Lower Deck with a seven piece honky-tonk band. Spoons and all! Of course we decided to venture forth and lo and behold, to our surprise, we discovered an entire colony of octogenarians dancing and drinking and acting kind of like we do. Mind you, they were way better at dancing and weren't afraid to tell us so, either. They even gave us a few lessons. Oh, and have I mentioned that the beer prices don't even hit the three dollar mark? What more can you ask for? We actually made a few good friends there, despite the age gap, and one night we went and had a jam session with the band after the show. We like to go back now and then, but nothing will ever top that first night at the Lower Deck.

Run!
Alice Norquay

<u>Site-Specific Location</u>

Corner of Elm Street and Paris Street, in front of the mall

ALICE

Ugh. Finally. School shouldn't happen when it's nice out.

CHRISTIANE

At least we're done for the day.

ALICE

Yeah… what are we gonna do now?

CHRISTIANE

Bus somewhere, I guess. As long as we don't get peed on again.

ALICE

What do you mean "peed on"? I only remember seeing that guy pee outside at the bus depot.

CHRISTIANE

Well, I had another guy get surprised, turn around and pee on my shoe!

ALICE

(laughs) That's awesome and also really gross. Anyway, we could just hang out here. Are we meeting Keith?

CHRISTIANE

I don't think so. Do you have your cell? You could call him.

ALICE

Forgot it this morning. There's a pay phone at the bus station though.

CHRISTIANE

Okay. Am I still staying over tonight?

ALICE

Yeah, I'll see if Keith is meeting us for breakfast, too.

CHRISTIANE
Us? I thought you said you didn't want to meet for breakfast anymore. You're too scared you'll be late.

ALICE
I'm not scared to be late!

CHRISTIANE
Well, the fact that you run up all the green stairs and almost pass out at the end of it, just so you won't be late, kind of says the opposite.

ALICE
I'm just not slow like you and Keith!

CHRISTIANE
Pff. Hey! Marymount girls! Run!

ALICE
(laughs) You know they call us the CND misfits. Seriously, I was like, "Raise your hand if you're allowed to have boys at your school. Who's the misfits now?" The girls on my bus are ridiculous.

CHRISTIANE
Alice, I think they heard you. Run! Before we catch snob from them!

ALICE
(screams) Oh no! I actually think they heard us! Go! Go! Go! *(running)*

CHRISTIANE
Are we seriously running from them?

ALICE
(laughs) We seriously are. This is stupid.

CHRISTIANE
Door! Door!

ALICE
Open it! Open it!

Glass shatters.

Did you just kick the door?

CHRISTIANE
Ummm…

ALICE
Did you just honestly kick the door?

CHRISTIANE
Ummm…

ALICE
You just shattered that glass!

CHRISTIANE
Ummm… RUN!

Joe Morrow

Robin Sokoloski founded and manages the Uᵗʰ Ink: Playwrights in the Community program. She is a dynamic participant in Toronto's community art scene. Robin is the administrative coordinator for the Canadian Youth Arts Network (CYAN) and is a board member of Lakeshore Arts, a local art service organization. In 2004 she developed a youth art program entitled Youth Arts Movement (YAM) that sets out to create youth programming from a youth perspective. It was for this endeavour that she was the winner of Humber College's Board of Governors' Achievement Award. Robin is the Outreach and Communications Manager at Playwrights Guild of Canada and currently lives with Joe, her husband to be and her dog, Kaya.